Keisha & Trigga
Reloaded
The Love Of A Gangsta

LEO SULLIVAN
PORSCHA STERLING

© 2016
Published by Leo Sullivan Presents

JOIN OUR MAILING LIST!

Text **LEOSULLIVAN** to **22828** to join our mailing list!
To submit a manuscript for our review, email us at
submissions@leolsullivan.com

SYNOPSIS

This book is dedicated to the readers who support Leo Sullivan Presents & Royalty Publishing House and the authors who make up each of those teams. We appreciate you.

1

The moment Trigga stepped into the house, he knew something wasn't right. Although he'd been out of the street life for over five years, the same senses that had helped him to survive were still intact and, at the moment, they were all sending him signals that he needed to be alarmed.

"Keesh? Why all the damn lights off—"

As soon as Trigga flicked on the switch and illuminated the front foyer of the house, his narrowed eyes focused on the one thing that was out of place on the pure white tile. The massive trail of crimson red blood smeared across the taupe floor and painted down the hall as if someone had been dragged down the walkway while bleeding profusely. Grabbing at his waist, Trigga reached for his banger instinctually, but it wasn't there.

"Shit!" he cursed as he took off down the hallway, suddenly remembering that he'd stopped carrying it years ago. Living the family life had made him too relaxed, and he was now regretting it.

With his heart thumping rhythmically in his ears and his blood running cold in his veins, Trigga ran down the hall, hoping to God that he wouldn't see what he almost knew for certain he would. The amount of blood on the floor was too much. There was no way that whoever it belonged to could still be alive. His shoes made a steady smacking sound as he followed the trail to his bedroom, and that's when he felt two things in his chest that he prayed he'd never feel: panic and fear.

Shoving the door open, his eyes immediately fell on a scene that would haunt *him for the rest of his life. His wife, the only woman he'd ever loved, Keisha, was lying motionless on the floor, her cerise blood painting a morbid scene around her lifeless body. Her eyes were wide open, displaying the last emotion that she'd felt before she reached her dire end: fear.*

"God, no! Please, don't take her from me!" Trigga pled as he dropped to his knees and crawled toward her body. Her blood began to seep through his jeans, but the liquid was cold against his skin and chilled his soul.

Grabbing her up in his arms, Trigga held her close to his chest, but her skin was cold as ice. She was gone. There was nothing he could do. God had taken her from him in the cruelest of ways. She was alone when she took her last breaths, and he wasn't able to be there to protect her.

"Daddy..." a quivering voice called out beside him, and it was the only thing that could pull Trigga's attention away from Keisha's body.

"Cam?" Trigga called out and spiraled around toward the sound of his son's voice.

Five-year-old Cameron made a grunting noise and then began to gurgle up blood between painful coughs as he tried with great effort to answer his father. With tears in his eyes, Trigga placed Keisha down gently and ran over to his son's side, completely covered in her blood.

"Cam... Shit! Cam, listen to me! You're gonna be a'ight," Trigga told him as his eyes searched his son's small body.

But a quick assessment told him that Cam was not going to be alright. From what Trigga could see, he had three bullet holes in his chest, and he was spitting out blood through his thin lips. Dubiously, Cameron struggled to nod his head as he looked into his father's face with the kind and gentle eyes that he'd gotten from his mother. Eyes that mirrored the same fear that she'd had in hers when she died.

Grabbing his son into his arms, Trigga held him tightly and listened to his weakening heartbeat as Cameron continued to cough up blood. Trigga had seen this many times before with many different people. There was no need to call for help because there was no time. The entire life that Cameron should have been able to live was now reduced down to seconds. The time was near, and there was no denying it; the only thing left to do was hold his son one last time before it was time for him to go.

"Cameron, I love you, man," Trigga told him as tears fell gingerly down his cheeks. He held him tight and repeated his love to his son over and over until his body went limp in his arms. But Trigga still didn't let go. He continued to hold his son and cry for the family he'd lost until Cameron's body, like his mother's, grew cold.

~

THE SOUND of movement next to him woke Trigga up from the reoccurring dream that he'd been having for the last week, and, once again, Keisha was already awake and staring straight at him. The dim lighting from the crescent moon coming through their translucent curtains highlighted the soft features in her face, but also brought light to the worry in her eyes.

"Trigga, this is like the fifth time this week that your ass has booted me out the damn bed in the middle of the night. Why in the world are you fighting and shit in your sleep?" she asked, rubbing the side of her arm with her face pulled into a tight frown, but her eyes still showed the concern she felt. Something was bothering him in his dreams, but every time she asked, he wouldn't say anything about it.

"I'm good, Keesh. It was that stew shit that you cooked for dinner last night. It's fuckin' with a nigga's stomach. What I told you about trying to cook?" he joked, rolling around in bed so that he could look at the clock.

As soon as he turned back around, he was greeted by a pillow straight to the head. Knocking it away, he started to laugh as he looked into Keisha's pouting face.

"Stop pouting, wit'cho soft ass," he said, still laughing as he stood up and stretched. "I'ma head down to the gym real quick, and then I'll be up to get Cam ready to go to school. You goin'?"

"Of course I'm going!" Keisha replied, jumping up out of bed. "You think I'ma miss his first day? Shit, after all the pain I went through bringing your big head ass son into the world, you should already know I'm not about to miss a thing."

Walking past him, Keisha wasn't the least bit surprised when she felt Trigga smack her on the ass before she slipped into their master bathroom. But she was surprised when Trigga walked in behind her and leaned on the wall, staring at her right as she was about to pull off her silk top.

"What you doing?" Keisha asked with crinkled brows as she began to take her clothes off.

"Just looking at you," he replied, his gray eyes glistening under the dim lights in the bathroom. She was beautiful to him, and he needed this image of her to erase what was still planted in his mind from his dream.

Smirking, Keisha bent over, making sure to keep her ass high in the air as she peeled off her panties and seductively shimmied them down her legs. Then she ran her hands over her body before turning around and sashaying over to the shower, bending low again to turn on the water.

Trigga smiled as he watched her begin her show, exaggerating every motion to appeal to his watchful stare. Turning toward him, she made a dramatic show of pulling off her hair tie and shaking her hair loose before pinching her nipples. But when Trigga reached out and grabbed at her, she snatched away and dodged him just in time before jumping into the shower.

"We don't have time for that. Gotta get Cam ready for his first day," she told him as she snatched the curtain closed, blocking his view of her curvaceous body.

She'd gained weight over the years since having Cameron, but she was still fine as fuck in his mind. And he was even more in love with her at that moment than he'd ever been before. In his mind, no woman could touch Keisha, and anyone who tried to steal his attention was reminded of such. He didn't play around when it came to her, and everyone knew that.

That said, they were going through a lot of issues and it often left him to wonder if Keisha really knew how much he loved her. They'd recently lost a child and Keisha still struggled with the lost and feeling like her past drug abuse was the reason for it. Deep down, she felt like Trigga blamed her although he always said he didn't.

"You full of shit, yo," Trigga responded, shaking his head as he walked out of the bathroom. "You lucky I wanna work out first, or I'd snatch your thick ass right out of there."

"Nigga, you ain't gon' do shi—"

Before she could finish her sentence, Trigga had snatched back the curtains and grabbed her by her waist, throwing her dripping wet body over his shoulder. Keisha squealed and giggled as he walked back into the bedroom and threw her onto the bed.

"What the fuck was all that shit you was talkin', Keesh?" he asked as he pulled down his boxers and released his manhood, which was already standing at attention, thanks to the mini striptease she'd given him a few minutes before.

Lips slightly parted, Keisha's eyes dropped down to his erection, but she didn't say a word. It excited Trigga even more. He leaned over her and parted her legs, then in one quick, single motion, he entered her and took her breath away. Rolling her hips in a circular motion, Keisha grinded into him in a way that she knew he loved and couldn't resist. She relaxed and let go... it almost felt like old times. His face twisted up with pleasure as he grabbed her around her waist and tried to slow her down, but she wouldn't let him.

"Shit, Keesh... slow the fuck down!" Trigga asked, but she didn't listen.

Finally, Trigga pulled all the way out and flipped her onto her stomach, before pushing forcefully into her again.

"You think I'ma let you fuck me?" he asked, pulling her hair around his fist to deepen the arch in her back as she moaned out in pleasure. "Naw, you gon' bow down to this dick."

And with that, Trigga sped up his motion as he held on to her waist, making her throw it back even more vigorously as he impaled her with his rod. Finally, he felt her muscles begin to contract as she came to a climax, and that's when he let go and exploded into her, breathing heavily as he enjoyed the feel of their juices mixing together inside of her.

"Damn," Keisha cursed as she rolled over on the bed and stared at him, her eyes drunkenly drooping from the exhilarating after effect of his love. "I'm ready to go back to sleep now."

"Get your ass up so you can make some breakfast for our son," Trigga ordered, tapping her lovingly on the ass. "Nothing too difficult. Maybe some cereal or some shit. I don't want you fuckin' up my lil' man's stomach on his first day."

"Trigga!" Keisha snapped as she watched him wink at her and walk into the bathroom to clean up. "You so muthafuckin' rude! I swear I hate your ass!"

"I know," he replied as he began to shut the door behind him, a sly smirk forming on his face. "That's why a nigga gotta eat at the club now. Your hateful ass be taking out your negativity on a nigga's meals and shit."

Before fully closing the door behind him, he peeked back out at Keisha.

"Aye, you coming to the club tonight with me?" he asked. Keisha yawned before responding.

"No...I have something else I have to tend to," she said with ease but her face didn't match her tone.

She seemed put off and tense as she spoke and her eyes avoided his. Trigga caught it but didn't question her any further, assuming it was some 'woman shit' that she was trying to spare him of hearing.

"Okay...just wondering because you been skipping out on a few nights. I know the girls would love to see you," he added as he continued to watch her expression shift. Keisha rolled her eyes and threw a pillow at him. He used the door to block it.

"No, they would like to see *you*," she corrected him. "Them hoes don't think about me at all unless it's to talk shit about how they can't stand when I come around so they can't bounce their asses in your face."

Trigga watched as Keisha pulled her face into a pout and laughed before closing the door behind him. The girls at the club were how he made his money, nothing more, and Keisha knew that. When it came to him, she knew she never had to worry about another woman taking what he'd pledged to her.

2

"*W*hat's that?" Keisha asked as she watched Trigga stuff something in the back of his waist before pulling his shirt down to cover it. "That's not a gun, is it?"

Pulling his eyebrows into a straight line, Trigga didn't readily respond, but gave Keisha a look that told her everything she needed to know.

"Is something wrong? You haven't carried a weapon since Cam turned three," she inquired further, dropping down onto the bed as she watched him pull on his shoes.

Trigga pushed his lips firmly together. For a second, he considered the idea of telling her about the dream, but then quickly pushed the idea from his mind. Call it superstition, but he felt that speaking it made it real, and he refused to give life to the murder of his wife and child.

"Something has been going on with you for the past couple weeks, and you need to talk to me," Keisha pressed further. "Is it because this month would have been Sade's fourth birthday? It's been bothering me too but—"

Keisha stopped when she saw the way Trigga's face twisted up. Just that quickly, their blissful morning had ended.

Trigga felt a knot form in his throat at the mention of Sade, their daughter who had died only hours after her premature birth. Keisha thought he blamed her for their baby's death but it wasn't true. He was the one to blame. He still faulted himself for what happened to her, and what Keisha was saying was true. Every year on her birthday, he went into a depression and mourned for the child they had lost. Deep down, Trigga felt like all the complications that Keisha experienced during pregnancy was his fault. She was still suffering from the life that he'd put her through when they'd met.

"I'm good, Keesh. I just want to make sure my family is protected. I've gotten a little relaxed and forgot that you and Cam are all I got left. I need to do my part to make sure that y'all are good," he told her, honestly. A forced smile invaded his face but it didn't reach his eyes and the light was gone from them.

Keisha gave him a look that let him know she only halfway believed what he was saying, but before she could pursue her inquiry any further, Cameron ran into the room with a ring of milk around his mouth. Lifting his arm, he went to wipe it off with the sleeve of his shirt.

"Boy, you bet not wipe that milk off on your clothes!" Keisha yelled, going into full Mommy mode, which made a genuine smile cross Trigga's face. "Get a napkin and clean your mouth."

Cameron's eyes dropped in remorse from being yelled at by his mother, but when he looked at the smile on his father's face, he couldn't stop himself from smiling in return. Trigga made a funny face at him, making Cameron fall out laughing. Keisha rolled her eyes at both of them. Cameron was an exact replica of Trigga but had his mother's complexion and her gentle personality. His stubbornness and carefree attitude came straight from Trigga.

"Okay, Mommy," Cameron replied before running out to do as he was told.

Frowning, Keisha turned to Trigga, who ducked his head and pretended to not see her glare.

"I can't be the only disciplinarian, Trigga... why you always playing around?" she asked, picking up a pillow and pelting him across the top of his head when he continued to act like he didn't hear her.

Ducking out of the way, Trigga grabbed the pillow and pulled, making Keisha lose her balance and fall onto his lap. Before she could move off, he started popping her on her ass as he held her in place.

"I... done... told... your...disrespectful... ass... about... hittin'... me... with them... fuckin' pillows!" Trigga playfully scolded her, popping her on her firm ass with each word until Keisha finally wiggled out of the way.

Standing up, Keisha fixed her skirt and then shot Trigga a look before mushing him in the head.

"I hate your rude ass!" she scoffed, making Trigga laugh at her pretending to be angry, but he knew she liked it.

"Let's go before you make Cam late on his first day."

As soon as the words left Trigga's mouth, there was a knock at the door. He and Keisha exchanged looks, confirming that neither of them was expecting anyone to stop by.

"Daddy, somebody's at the door!" Cameron chimed out from the living room as soon as Trigga walked out of the bedroom.

Pursing his lips together, Trigga nodded at him and then walked over to the door. He had a strange feeling in his stomach as parts of his dream began to come back to him, visions that he never wanted to see again, whether it be in real life or even in a dream. His eyes went to the window next to the door, and he could see the shadow of a large figure standing at the door, which made his hand automatically travel to the banger stashed at his back. He hadn't had to bust on a nigga in nearly five years, but he wouldn't hesitate to do so if it came to protecting his family.

When he looked out the peephole, Trigga cursed under his breath at the big ass man who stood at the door with the build of Mike Tyson in his day. He had on a black shirt and black pants, but, even through his clothes, Trigga's trained eye could see that he had about four weapons stashed on him. His face was pulled into a serious expression that told anyone looking at him that he was ready to go at any time.

Baring his teeth, Trigga turned the locks and snatched the door open, preparing himself for the load of bullshit standing at his front door. But whatever was about to happen, he was ready for it.

3

"**N**igga, what you doin' here?" he asked, although he already knew the answer to his question.

"C'mon, Trigga, you know Queen ain't 'bout to let Cam have his first day of Kindergarten and she ain't here to see it," Rodney responded, cocking his head to the side, he gave Trigga a sideways look.

"Maaaaaaan, fuck!" Trigga cursed as he looked at the fleet of black vehicles in front of his house. "I told her to tone this shit down after what she did for his first day of pre-k! She got it looking like the damn secret service and the president up in this bitch. I want Cam to be low-key... all this shit is too much!"

"I had a feeling you were going to say that," Queen said with a sigh as she walked up from the side.

Trigga had been so distracted by all the cars stacked up in his driveway and on his lawn, that he hadn't even seen her standing there. For some reason, the fact that he hadn't been aware of her presence before she made it known annoyed him. He had been out of the street game for some time now and any reminder that he was getting rusty frustrated him.

"I don't want all this attention brought to him. Niggas see this shit, and they start lookin' at him differently. You should know what I mean. Isn't that why you homeschool Rome and Italy?"

Queen thought about his words for a few minutes before turning to Rodney.

"Trigga's right. Cam is going to public school, so we actually may need to add a few more cars. And, Rodney, I think you should be stationed outside of his classroom throughout the school day to make sure he's safe while he's not under his parents' supervision," she told her guard, who gave Trigga a gloating look when he saw him clench his jaw at Queen's words.

Before Trigga could say anything, Queen started to laugh.

"Trigga, I'm kidding. Can't you take a joke?" she asked him as Keisha walked out the front door and stood next to him. "Keisha, can you teach your husband how to take a joke?"

"Humph," Keisha grunted, cutting her eyes at Trigga. "If you ask me, his ass has been joking all morning." It was obvious she was still feeling some kind of way about what happened earlier.

Then, turning to Queen, she said, "Queen, I thought that we agreed after what happened for pre-k that—"

"We can all go in one of the cars. The others will trail us, but stop once we get near the school," she said in a way that was more of a statement than a question, which was her normal fashion. Queen didn't ask permission for anything. It wasn't in her nature.

Queen turned to Cameron, who was peeking outside from the side of the door. As soon as he saw his godmother, his entire face lit up, and he ran over to her with his arms wide. Queen bent down and scooped him into her arms.

"You ready for your first day of school, big man?" Queen asked him, and Cameron nodded his head.

While Keisha's eyes were focused on the rare display of affection that Queen saved only for Cameron, Trigga's stare shifted to their surroundings. He had a strange feeling that they were being watched. A quick glance around told him that it was most likely paranoia based on his recurring nightmare. He shook off the feeling as quickly as it had come, but not before running his hand over the strap tucked behind his back.

"A'ight, let's get out of here," he told them, cutting the conversation short after checking his watch. "We can't let Cam be late on his first day."

"Right, plus I have a few appointments this morning," Keisha added, checking her watch.

Everyone nodded their head, and they walked toward the SUV that Queen had selected for them. Trigga knotted his brows as he stared at Keisha intensely. More appointments she hadn't said a word about. He made a mental note to bring it up at another time.

Trigga reached down and grabbed Cameron's hand firmly in his, feeling a new wave of apprehension at having to get used to the fact that, for once, since he'd been born, Cameron would be out the sight of everyone who had protected him since he was born.

IT WAS ONLY EARLY AFTERNOON, but that didn't mean anything to the patrons of *The Lair*, Trigga's strip club. The club opened at noon, and it was just as packed around the early hours as it was during the late night, however it was still operating at a loss. *The Lair*, once open 24/7, had to cut down its hours due to business being slow during certain times of the day. Although it seemed busy at the moment, the shortened hours affected the overall income, but Trigga had ideas for how to bridge the gap, and it was already working.

"Aye, Trigga, we got somebody waiting who came in to see you," B.J., the bartender and club manager, told him as soon as he walked in. He nodded his head behind Trigga's back, toward where Trigga assumed the person he was referring to was sitting.

Immediately, Trigga's eyes fell upon a woman sitting in the middle of the club by herself, her gentle, doe-like eyes firmly planted on his face. Upon visually connecting with Trigga, a light passes through her eyes and her lips curl at the edges into a small smile.

"Talent?" Trigga asked, pulling his attention from her and back to B.J., who nodded his answer with a shrug.

"Yeah, says she just moved here from somewhere out west and needs a job. She claims she's a student and all that normal shit... working to get the money to be a nurse, and blah, blah, blah... you know that shit that all the bitches say. She showed me a video of her performance at her other club, and shawty is definitely official. You should take a look."

The devilish smirk on B.J.'s toffee-colored face told Trigga everything he needed to know regarding what he personally felt about the woman sitting behind them. B.J. was the manager of the club, but also a not-so-reformed playboy who was able to easily pull any woman he set his attention on by using his good looks. Even though he was well into his fifties, he had no issues pulling women like a man half his age.

With his large but gentle brown eyes, smooth complexion, athletic build, and deep, late night radio host voice, even Keisha had to admit that he was definitely easy on the eyes, but Trigga had made it clear to him that the workers in the club were off-limits. However, he was sure that B.J. still did whatever he wanted to do but just managed to keep it on the low.

"Give me a minute to get situated, and I'll tell you when you can send her in," Trigga told him dismissively before grabbing his cell phone that was vibrating in his pocket.

I just called the school to check on Cam, but no one answered. Maybe I should stop by there? Keisha texted, making him smile. He chuckled a little to himself before replying to her message.

Relax, Keesh. They can't teach him shit if you keep calling down there. He's fine, he responded and then put his phone back into his pocket as he walked into his office.

As soon as he stepped inside, he felt the looming presence of someone behind him. Ignoring the prickly sensation rising up on his neck, he turned around just as he heard B.J.'s voice yell out, "Hey!". Behind Trigga, standing with an expectant but warm look on her face, was the woman who had been sitting at the table when he walked in.

Now that she was standing close to him, he was able to get a good look at her, and he could see why B.J. had been looking at him the way he had when he mentioned her. She had a cool brown complexion that seemed to shimmer in the light. Her big eyes were bright and oval-shaped and pointed upwards at the end in a way that made it seem like she was smiling on the inside as she stared at him.

Her pouty lips were perfectly shaped and complimented her high cheek-bones. If Trigga had to guess at her ancestry, he would say Ethiopian. She had beautiful, dark brown skin with short, naturally curly hair that framed her doll-like face. She had a way of looking into his eyes with a pointed stare that made it seem as if she knew more about him than she should, giving him a false sense of comfort with her that bothered him. Trigga snickered on the inside a bit as he looked at her and thought about Keisha.

Keisha is not going to like this chick, Trigga thought.

Although Keisha had been given no reason for it, it was widely known that she was jealous when it came to Trigga. She had no problem checking any and everybody whom she thought posed a threat to her in his club.

"Hey!" B.J. said once more as he finally caught up with the woman, who was standing at the entrance of Trigga's office. Standing beside her, he bent down, placing his hands on his knees and let out a long breath between staggered gasps.

"I told you to wait until he got here!"

"I did. He's here," was her simple, yet very direct response. Although she wasn't rude, it came out very direct

Watching carefully, Trigga started to assess her in the way that he did everyone he came into contact with. It was a personality trait that he'd carried with him from his days in the streets. Her gentility stopped at her looks. Her attitude was bold, borderline aggressive, and she exuded confidence. Her soft and innocent look would help her with the club patrons who preferred a woman who seemed to portray those characteristics, but her aggressiveness would make her a lot of money, and Trigga knew it.

"She's good," he told B.J. with a nod of his head before walking behind his desk and sitting down. He motioned for her to take a seat on the chair in front of him.

"A'ight, I'm up front if you need me," B.J. replied, giving a narrowed look at the woman, showing that he wasn't at all happy with the fact that she'd usurped his authority.

"Thanks for meeting with me," she started as Trigga searched aimlessly through some papers on his desk. "I'm Lania, and I'm from Texas, and—"

Lania stopped when Trigga lifted a piece of paper in front of his face. With his thick brows bunched into a frown, he began reading it, ignoring her presence completely. Afterwards, he grabbed his phone out of his pocket and started pecking away on it without saying a word. An annoyed scowl painted itself across Lania's face as she watched Trigga continue to go out of his way to ignore her.

"Um..."

Trigga cut her off by clearing his throat and then kicked his feet up on the desk and grabbed a magazine before starting to flip through it slowly.

"Excuse me, I'm—"

"You're waiting for me to start the interview," Trigga said, finally pulling his eyes away from the pages of the magazine. "Which you could have done out there while you were entertained by the other girls who are presently employed. But you decided to walk back here on your own so you can wait until I'm ready to begin."

He's rude, Lania thought, frowning her face at Trigga as he went back to his magazine.

Wrinkling her face, Lania resisted the urge to fold her arms and pout at being treated in a way that she wasn't used to. She was used to men bowing to her good looks, but Trigga didn't seem the least bit taken by her looks. She scrutinized him slowly as he continued to peruse through the pages of the magazine in his hands as if she wasn't sitting there. His attitude didn't surprise her all that much, even though she was shocked that he'd directed his abrasive nature *at her*. She'd already heard all about Trigga and knew that he wasn't a regular man who was easily affected by a beautiful woman. But out of all the things she heard about him, one thing that she hadn't heard was how sexy he was.

He's probably used to having the attention of bad bitches on the daily, she thought to herself as she wet her lips and continued to let her eyes move over his stern face and hard body.

He was like sin in the flesh. Looking at him made her think of all the things she would allow him to do to her if she had the chance. Her pulse started to thrum, setting her body on fire as she ran her eyes over the tattoos on his arms. Tattoos were her thing. Her eyes slid up to his chiseled, strong jawline. Everything about him was so masculine and so sexy.

The sound of heels clacking against the tile floor in the hall snatched Lania from the daydream that had begun in her mind as she ran her eyes once more over Trigga's muscular and perfectly chiseled biceps.

When Lania lifted her head, she saw that she was looking directly into his cool gray eyes, and her cheeks flushed red under her milk chocolate skin. He'd caught her staring at him, which wasn't enough to embarrass her, but his unreadable expression was. She couldn't tell whether he was intrigued by her obvious appreciation of his good looks or put off by it. The awkward air between them spread steadily, making her shift in her chair.

"I'm here," a female voice said from the doorway, and Lania was appreciative of the disruption, hoping that it would calm the tension in the room between her and Trigga.

Before she could turn toward the source of the voice, a hand appeared next to her shoulder. Lania looked at it before following it up to the woman it belonged to; a very attractive female with a butterscotch complexion, straight black hair cut into a bob, and dark brown eyes that stared at her with a steeled expression in them.

"I'm Keisha, Trigga's wife," Keisha introduced herself, trying to keep a straight face as she focused on the beautiful woman before her.

"I'm Lania, but people call me Nia," Lania told her, shaking her hand. She forced a smile, only allowing her eyes to lock with Keisha's for a short second.

Turning around, Lania cut her eyes to Trigga, who seemed to be enjoying how uncomfortable she probably looked. He hadn't said a word, but the glimmer in his eyes suggested that he knew she wished she could carve out a hole into the ground and fall into it. As soon as Keisha pulled away from Lania, he stood up and motioned for Keisha to take his seat. When she walked by him, he grabbed her around her waist and pulled her into a deep kiss.

Lania kept her eyes on Trigga as he cupped Keisha's ass in his hands during their embrace, and couldn't help the smirk that crossed her face. He was sending a clear message that he wanted her to stay away. The question that crossed her mind was whether he wanted her to stay away because he thought she was interested in him or because he'd actually found himself tempted by her. He seemed to be going out of the way to prove his loyalty to his wife. But was it for her benefit or his?

"I'll leave y'all to it," he told Keisha, without looking at Lania before he walked out and closed the door behind him.

Clearing her throat, Keisha sat down in Trigga's chair and brought her gaze to Lania's face, noting the fact that she'd unblinkingly watched Trigga's open display of affection. The fact that Trigga had even done it in the first place was sending off alarms in Keisha's mind about the woman who sat before her as she wondered what all had happened before she made her entrance.

I already don't like her ass, she thought to herself as she got a good look at Lania.

One thing was for sure, she was beautiful, but that wasn't enough for Keisha to decide that she didn't care for her. What she didn't like was that Lania seemed to be laughing behind her eyes as she sat in the chair and waited for Keisha to begin. Keisha was used to females being uncomfortable with her presence in the room, but this reaction was different, and she didn't like it.

Each dancer that came in was more beautiful than the last and used to getting men to do whatever they pleased based on their looks. As soon as they found out that Trigga was happily married, their body language would change as they began to realize that the nature of their relationship with him was definitely all business. Lania was different. Although she had seemed unsure of herself when Keisha initially walked in, that was a far cry to how confident and bold she appeared now.

"You can start by telling me about yourself," Keisha began with pursed lips. This interview was a waste of time. If it were up to her, Lania wouldn't be working at Lair.

"Why don't you start telling me about you first?" Lania replied curtly. "I've heard a lot about Trigga, but I've never heard anything about a wife."

"Excuse me?" Keisha asked with a raised brow. Her cheat tightened and the air prickled around them as the tension grew.

"What I mean is," Lania started as she sensed she was walking on dangerous ground. "You're interviewing me instead of him, which I wasn't prepared for. So, I guess I'd be working under you, and I just like to know a little bit about who I'll be working for."

Biting her bottom lip, Keisha paused before answering.

"Well, as Trigga's wife, I am part owner of the club, as well as the bartender here some nights. Other nights, I'm home with *our son*. You have any other questions?" Keisha gritted while tapping her pen against the top of the desk.

With her soft eyes wide, Lania shook her head gently, but Keisha was not put off at all by her sudden innocent act.

Standing up suddenly, she said, "We're done here."

Scrunching up her face, Lania frowned as she watched Keisha walk over and open the door. "What do you mean?" she asked. "You didn't give me any questions."

"We're good. You can leave, and if you need your parking ticket validated, B.J. can do it for you," Keisha told her, gesturing towards the door.

Standing up, Lania gave her a hardened stare before sashaying down the hall toward the main part of the club as Keisha watched her. Right when Lania was about to bend the corner, she turned around and gave Keisha an apologetic look that made her stomach churn. Her spirit was telling her that the woman was trouble, but there was something else about her that was unsettling to Keisha.

The look in Lania's eyes and her demeanor reminded her of something in herself that died the moment she relinquished her feelings for Lloyd and stopped being his side bitch in order to be Trigga's woman. Lania had that same aura and careless attitude about her that Keisha had, knowing that she was fucking around with a man who was married to another woman.

Unfortunately, although Lania was out of her sight for the moment, Keisha had the haunting feeling that she hadn't seen the last of her.

4

Grinding her back teeth against each other, a single bead of sweat sprouted at Keisha's hairline as she held her breath and attempted yet another time to button the top of a pair of skinny jeans that hadn't fit quite as snug weeks before.

"Arrrgh!" she growled as she tugged and tried to bring the opening of her jeans together around the newly formed pudginess at her waist.

Breathing heavily, she released the jeans and pulled at her top as she wondered for a minute if she could get away with leaving the jeans unbuttoned. The bulge in front of her told her, no, and she began to angrily kick the jeans off right as Trigga walked into the bedroom.

As soon as Trigga saw the frustrated look etched across her face as she booted the jeans with her foot, making them sail across the floor, he made an about-face to exit the room. Over the last few weeks, Keisha had gained a considerable amount of weight, and he already knew what the business was as soon as he walked in and witnessed her assault on her own clothing.

"TRIGGA!" Keisha yelled, stopping him before he could get too far down the hall.

His eyes closed on a long blink and he exhaled sharply and turned back toward the room. "Keesh, don't even ask me what I know you're about to ask me because last time you—"

"Do I look fat to you?" she inquired with her head cocked to the side and her arms wide as she stood only in a long shirt and panties.

It's a trap, the seasoned voice in Trigga's mind warned him, but he exhaled and sat down on the bed as he stared into Keisha's eyes.

"No, you look beautiful to me," he replied truthfully, hoping she would drop the subject. But, of course, she didn't.

"But I've gained a few pounds lately... I mean, would you rather I looked like the chicks down at the club?"

"The strippers?" Trigga frowned. "Hell naw! Bae, I'm happy with what I got. Them females don't do nothing for me."

"Yeah, but you hire them based on their looks, so you must find them attractive... would you want me to look more like them?"

Sensing the trap that Keisha was unknowingly laying for him, Trigga sat up and shook his head.

"Listen, we aren't even about to get into that shit," he told her. "Have you gained a little weight? Yes, you have—" Keisha winced. "—But I don't care about that shit! Stop worrying about them chicks down at the club because when it comes to me, they ain't got shit on you. You're the mother of my son, and we've been through some crazy shit together.

You've proven that you'll die for me... we've built something together that no one can compare to. A little bit of weight and a few stretch marks—" Keisha winced again. "—That shit don't mean anything to me because I know where it came from. You carried our children, and that is just evidence of your sacrifice. Stop worrying about that little shit."

Trigga's blunt declaration took every ounce of worry she had away in an instant. Keisha sauntered over to him and fell into his arms, feeling herself melt instantly into him as he held her, running a trail of kisses down her neck.

"You gotta stop," Keisha moaned gently when he reached down at started kneading her treasure box through the thin lace of her panties. "Cam might walk in here."

"That nigga is knocked out," Trigga replied before slipping his fingers around the material that kept him separated from her most sensitive area. "A whole week of school with no naps has caught up to his ass. Plus...I need this. It's been a while."

Falling into him, Keisha moaned gently against him, her knees nearly buckling when he pushed two fingers inside of her and began to stir her honeypot. Trigga bit gently on her neck as he cupped her ass with his other hand and moved her on top of the dresser behind her. Once he sat her down, Keisha fell back and let the wall support her as Trigga pushed her legs open and dove right between them, tongue first. He latched his lips onto the swollen nub between her thighs and sucked eagerly, slurping up all of her nectar.

Keisha began to grind her hips against him as he continued to work his tongue inside of her, hungry for everything that she was willing to give him. Within seconds, her body was shivering. Bringing her hand to the back of his head, she grinded even more into him as he continued to sip from her until she reached her climax. She bit down hard on her fingers to stop herself from shouting out loud in pleasure.

After she'd come, Trigga kissed her clit and then stood up, wiping his mouth with the back of his hand. Keisha's drooping eyes confirmed what he already knew was about to happen when he'd started.

Her ass is about to go to sleep.

"Aye, you can stay home tonight," Trigga told her as he helped her up from the dresser. "B.J.'s there, and he can handle the crowd."

"But I haven't worked any since Cam started school," Keisha retorted with a yawn as she steadied herself on her feet. Her knees were still trembling slightly.

"Yeah, I know, and that's okay," Trigga told her. "Just rest up. We got it handled at the club."

Nodding her head, Keisha walked over and fell right into the bed as Trigga watched her. Within seconds, she was fast asleep. Bowing out of the room, he closed the door behind him, thankful for more than one reason that she had decided to stay home instead of coming into work that day.

"So WHEN YOU GON' tell Keisha that the bitch she kicked out your office is our headliner?" B.J. asked with a shit-starting grin on his face, leaning over the counter of the bar as Trigga sat sipping from a glass of Crown and Coke.

After draining the glass, Trigga dropped it on the countertop and pushed it toward B.J., who started to pour him a refill, but Trigga raised his hand to stop him.

"I'm good," he told him. "And so is Keisha. She gets in her feelings sometimes, but she knows this shit is all business, and she's not gonna stop money from being made, the same way I won't."

B.J. cut his eyes to where Lania was on the stage seductively humping in a slow and skillful way. Every person in the crowd, male or female, was going wild, their eyes plastered to every single curve on her perfect body. He then turned to Trigga, who seemed to be making a point to let his eyes look everywhere but on the stage.

Being a playboy meant that B.J. could read the ladies, but he could read men just as well, and he knew that Trigga making an effort not to pay attention to Lania meant more than if he had been openly ogling her as she sashayed her ass across the stage. Trigga passed her messages through B.J., and on the rare occasions that he did speak to her, he made sure to not let his eyes fall below her neckline. With every other dancer in the club, Trigga was comfortable and at ease in his interaction, but B.J. had noticed that things were different when it came to Lania. Although he wasn't sure why, he wasn't willing to bite his tongue when it came to finding out.

"So, what you think about shawty?" B.J. asked Trigga as Lania finished up her second number on the stage. The stage was covered with dollars. In a matter of days, she'd gone from being the newbie to the club's headliner.

"Who?" Trigga asked. Although he knew who B.J. was referring to, he wasn't sure he wanted to go down that road with him.

"Lania....Nia, whatever her name is. What do you think about her?" B.J. brought clarity to his question as he poured a drink for a man who had just sat down at the bar and placed his order.

"I don't," was Trigga's response, which brought a taunting smirk to B.J.'s lips.

"What?!" Trigga asked, a little too loudly when he saw the smug look on B.J.'s face.

"That's my point. You're cool with all the other chicks working here. Even Yadi, who Keisha has made it obvious that she can't stand. Yet, you make a point of being distant and cold when it comes to Lania, which seems odd to me," he explained further. He placed his elbows on the countertop and leaned down, supporting his chin with his hands as he waited for Trigga to respond.

"The difference between Lania and someone like Yadi is that Yadi knows her place. Lania is the type of bitch who is just waiting to catch a nigga slipping so she can swing through. She's good for business, which is why I keep her here, but I know better than to pay her thirsty ass any attention," Trigga told him with a shrug. He adjusted his clothing and B.J. watched, still smiling.

"She doesn't seem thirsty at all to me. Barely pays any real attention to you beyond what she should since you're her boss and all...even though you don't act like it," B.J. added with a lifted brow. "Just be careful. I used to swing through hoes even though I had a main chick, back in the day, but that type of life doesn't seem like it would suit you. You too...honest."

"And I love my wife," Trigga added with certainty as he shifted on his barstool.

"You tellin' me or yourself, youngin'?" B.J. countered with a pointed expression. "Because I already know."

Trigga suddenly became aware of someone staring at him and turned to look across the floor. His eyes focused on a dark figure situated in a corner booth near the back of the club. As he peered through the thick crowd and maintained his stare, he saw that it was a man sitting by himself. His dark eyes seemed to waver between Trigga and Lania, who was still twerking it out on the stage.

Trigga's hood senses went on alert. To him, the phantom man looked as if he were evaluating, estimating, thoughts speculating, plotting on something or someone.

Then, something very sinister dawned on Trigga as a seismic shiver ran down his spine. The neon lights flashed, shimmering a rainbow of colors bouncing around the club. The man's face looked familiar. Trigga was unable to ignore the gut-wrenching feeling stirring in his stomach. He kept his eyes on him, staring as if in a trance.

Where do I know that face from?

With an eerie feeling, he searched his mind, all the cluttered recesses of his dreary, dangerous past. The back ally shootouts, the deadly confrontations, the many men who he has put into the ground, as well as the few that may still seek his untimely demise.

Then it hit him like a ton of bricks, and he felt his knees nearly buckle. Instantly, he reached for the .9mm in his pants pocket. Something about the man reminded him of Lloyd. The same Lloyd that he had personally killed years ago.

5

"*I*t fuckin' can't be!" he exclaimed so loudly that a waitress walked over, thinking he was talking to her.

He fanned her off like an annoying fly. Just when he was about to walk over to the man in the corner, he felt a hand touch his shoulder. For some reason, Trigga flinched, spinning around and pulled out his banger, concealing it at his side.

"Hey, boss... can I talk to you for a minute?" a voice said above the pulsating base of a Drake and Rihanna song.

"What?!" Trigga grumbled with an attitude.

The voice belonged to Lania. She had a sheen of perspiration gleaming off her forehead as she stood there in the nude.

Trigga was annoyed, no frustrated was a better word. He quickly turned his head back around, and the man with the daunting, familiar face was gone.

"Is everything alright?" Lania asked in a timid voice. She had peeped the gun he furtively held at his side.

"Sure, what is it?" Trigga asked, not paying her the least bit of attention as he bobbed his head as if he were frantically searching for something or someone with the gun in his hand. For a fleeting moment, Lania wondered if Trigga could be under the influence of drugs as she watched him do a full 360 circle, looking around the packed club.

He noticed her looking at him with apprehension and dread smoldering in her eyes. He imagined what he must look like spinning with a banger in his hand, and he quickly played it off.

"Oh, sorry about that." With a subtle shrug and a polite smile, he gestured to the gun in his hand. "I thought I saw some trouble in the club. We don't want no one harassing the girls." He placed the gun back in his pocket, but his eyes continued to search their surroundings.

She frowned at him quizzically with an arched brow, and stood back on her bow legs, causing her ample breast to jiggle, nipples erect like strawberries in the summer time. He did his best not to look down. A feat no man has been able to accomplish when Lania was in her birthday suit.

"Can I talk to you?" she asked above the music and leaned forward causing a ringlet of hair to fall over on her forehead.

Instantly, he was engulfed with the redolence of her perfume. It seemed to gnaw at his resistance.

"Talk about what?" he asked and stole a glance down at her midriff, then tore his eyes away from her luscious body. Her vagina was bald as an eagle's ass, and she had some type of sexy tattoo paw prints walking away from her crotch, making a trek down her thigh.

"Can we go to your office or somewhere that I can get some privacy?" she asked with a stoic expression and eased closer.

As Trigga pondered her question, he scanned the club once more for the mystery man who had eluded him like smoke from a bottle. Just then, B.J. walked up. He had a bottle of Ciroc in one hand, and a fist full of money in the other. A towel was slung over his shoulder.

"You can talk to me here," Trigga said finally.

Lania cut her eyes at B.J. as if telepathically telling him to kick rocks. It was obvious he wasn't going anywhere, and there was no shame in his game. His eyes devoured every inch of her sumptuous curves as she gave him a repugnant stare. Her delicate eyebrows knotted across her face, a signal for him to beat it. He didn't budge. In fact, he leaned on the bar, getting comfortable, and boldly ogled her body from head to toe. Trigga got the distinct impression that there was something going on between them, but he couldn't put his finger on it.

She sucked in an exaggerated breath and let out a protracted deep sigh in agitation. B.J. enjoyed the sensuous swell of her pendulous breasts, her hourglass figure, along with the sexy tats and the risqué burgundy hair cascading over her left breast.

"Oh... hmmm... I was wondering if I could pick up some more hours... I have three children—" She fidgeted, determined to keep her composure.

"You got three children! You never told me that, I mean... uh, damn!" B.J. said, and tried to clean up his blunder as he suddenly stood straight up and tried to play it off. She had his full attention in more ways than one; he was even considering being a candidate for the step daddy job if she offered him one.

"Ma, you got mad respect from me," he told her with admiration while looking at her backside. "Bitches with no kids don't look as good as you. You got *three,* and you fine as fuck, dayum! You and them babies, if y'all need anything, just holla at'cha boy. I *got* you."

Lania pursed her lip at him with a frown. She wished he would leave.

Trigga couldn't help but smirk as his eyes roamed around the club, but even he was blown away. Not so much because she had three kids and had been able to maintain a nice shape because Keisha had carried two and been able to do the same. His surprise came from the fact that he had no idea she had a family she was taking care of. Trigga made it his business to know personal details like that about the other dancers, but he didn't know anything about Lania's background. What B.J. said was true, he had made a point of not getting cool with Lania, and this was evidence of that.

"Anyways..." Lania continued, shooting B.J. annoyed looks, but he only blew her a kiss in return. "...I just was wondering if I could work longer hours because I'm only on the schedule for four or five hours each night right now, and that's it. I take a few classes during the day, but they are all over before noon, and—"

"I'll put you on the schedule for more hours next week," Trigga replied, cutting her off. She could tell his mind was distant, someplace else, as if something were troubling him. He swiveled around in the barstool before standing up to walk away. When he felt a hand grab him by his wrist, he stopped suddenly.

"Look... is there a problem? I mean, like damn, you got issues with bitches from Texas?" Lania asked him pointedly.

She was growing tired of his distant attitude and the constant 'I'm-pissed-off' expression that he wore whenever he looked at her.

"What?" Trigga inquired and shook her hand loose from his arm then backed away slightly, increasing the gap between the two of them.

"Listen, I know we got off on the wrong foot and all, but it's been a week, and you treat me like I have a disease or something," Lania continued with a scowl on her face. "I make just as much money in here as the more experienced dancers, and I feel like I work twice as hard! I don't cause you any trouble, I'm here on time, I finish my set, I clean up my shit, and I leave. I've seen you joke and shit with the other bitches in here, but when I come around, you leave without greeting me with a simple 'hello.' Did I do something to you?"

Shocked into silence, Trigga's piercing gray eyes was trained on the annoyed expression on Lania's face. His eyebrows furrowed as he looked at her curiously and contemplated whether or not he owed her a response. He licked his lips with his dry tongue and became suddenly conscious of how dry his mouth was at the moment.

"No issues. We're good," he told her with a sigh, and watched, as she seemed to relax slightly.

"Good," Lania replied with a small smile gracing her face. "For a second, I thought you were acting some kind of way because of what happened between your wife and me."

Her sudden mention of Keisha made the hair rise up on Trigga's arm, and before he knew it, he felt himself getting heated, his anger rolling off of him like waves. Maybe it was because he had just called her and she hadn't picked up and sent him a text that she was on the other line. Who could she possibly be talking to this time of night that was more important than him?

"I've been waiting for her to come back in here so I could apologize to her,' Lania continued with an innocent smile. "I think she feels like I want you or some shit. You're sexy and shit, but—"

"The problem with you is that you don't know when to speak and when to shut the hell up," Trigga told her, his fists balled up at his sides. "Keisha isn't worried about any female in here because she doesn't have a reason to. I've never given her a reason to be worried about any female. What we have is worth more than dipping into average pussy."

Lania's brown eyes clouded over, and her face remained expressionless, but her anger was evident. She glanced over to the bar where B.J. was pouring drinks, out of earshot of their conversation. However, him being out of listening range did nothing to ease her fury as she turned her attention back to Trigga.

"Just like any self-confident and self-assured female, I feel free to speak my mind when I feel it's appropriate. I'm sorry if that bothers you, but I didn't see anything wrong or inappropriate with what I said, given the fact that I've been on that stage four times every night completely naked right in front of your face. But, either way... if I've crossed the line, I apologize," Lania added with a roll of the eyes before returning to her glare. "As far as my pussy is concerned, it's obviously not average because it brings in above average dollars... every single night."

Before giving Trigga the opportunity to respond, Lania turned on her heels and walked away. She wasn't able to get even three feet away before one of the club's top spenders cuffed her around the waist and whispered in her ear. Lania giggled in response before reaching for his hand and ushering him toward the private rooms. Before walking in, she shot Trigga a look as if to gloat on her last statement about how much money she brought in.

Gritting his teeth, Trigga's eyes surveyed the room when once again he began to feel as if someone was watching him. He turned toward the booth in the corner where the man from earlier had been, hoping he may have come back, and praying his mind was playing tricks on him. It had to be. Lloyd was dead, he had personally sent him to hell, a one way ticket, no return, no coming back, closed casket.

Then, how? Who was that sitting in that booth? His perplexed mind ruminated.

"Everything good, Tee?" Yadi asked, walking up on him with her large, bountiful bosom on full display. She had a large tattoo of a black Panther cat on her right shoulder with the head spanning across breasts. Her slender hips were laced with gold chains that just barely covered the space between her thighs as she swayed them from side to side to walk toward him.

"Yeah, I'm good," he replied, his eyes cutting to the private room that Lania had disappeared to.

For some reason that he couldn't explain, her words were still fucking with him.

"You sure?" Yadi inquired further. "I saw you talking to the new girl."

Yadi did nothing to hide her disdain for Lania or 'the new girl' as she preferred to call her, and Trigga instantly knew why. Before Lania, Yadi was the top earner, but her crown had been taken from her after Lania had only been employed for a few days.

"I'm good," Trigga repeated. "Aye, did you see the nigga in the back with the black and red on?" His eyes swooped the club once more as he searched for him.

Throwing her long, silky straight weave over her shoulder, Yadi sucked her teeth and then rolled her eyes before responding. "Yeah, I saw him, but he wasn't nothing but a cheap ass watcher. Didn't throw not one fuckin' bill. I hate niggas like that... come here to catch a fuckin' free show, and that's it."

"Okay, I was just wondering," Trigga told her. He was still unable to squash the feeling in his chest that he was being watched, but he didn't want to seem paranoid.

"I'll let you know if I see him again," Yadi promised, shooting him a smile before disappearing into the crowd.

Before long, same as Lania, a man had grabbed her round the waist and asked for a private dance. With a wide grin on her face, Yadi obliged, letting him run his hand over her wide ass as they walked toward the room.

Before he could catch himself, Trigga found his eyes traveling back to the door that Lania had disappeared behind and then checked his watch. She'd been in there for a while already. Her dance should have been nearing its end, but the door was still closed.

The fuck do I care? Trigga thought, shaking his head. It wasn't his place to clock the time on the dances.

I got bigger shit to do, he reminded himself as he surveyed the club one last time then walked back to his office.

His mind instantly fell back on the man who had been sitting in the back of the club there was something about him the reminded him of Lloyd.

6

A solitary light bulb hung from the eggshell white colored ceiling, engulfed in plumes of gray smoke billowing from the blunt being smoked by Trigga.

"Count it again?" Trigga asked for the third time.

"Look, man, I'm tired as shit. My feet, my back, and some mo' shit you don't wanna know about is hurting right now. Niggas lie, bitches lie, but numbers don't. Trigga, the count is the same. We just going to have to weather this storm," B.J. said.

"I'm just not getting it. How did we go from sugar to shit? Some nights we rake in a lot of dough, then there are nights we're actually losing money. Last month, I actually had to take some money out the bank to pay for the renovation of the VIP section and the lounge," Trigga said disgustedly, as he stared at the blunt in his hand.

"First off, it didn't help much that three other strip joints opened up in the past two years only a few miles away," B.J. said as he began to gather the money up.

"I know right. I think we may have underestimated our competition."

"Not we, YOU underestimated them! I been told you Foxy Ladies and The Gentlemen's Club were going to be a problem."

"Yes, but the Gentlemen's Club caters to white patrons. Dudes like seeing that black pussy twerkin'," Trigga commented.

"Like hell they do. Niggaz is on white pussy too, and for some reason, some of the girls have been leaving our spot and finding work there. Shit, the Gentlemen's Club be packed on a fucking Tuesday," B.J. commented with enthusiasm, then caught himself slipping.

Too late.

"How da fuck you know? You been in there?!" Trigga asked with steel in his voice.

"Hmmm, uh, maybe I been in there once or twice just to check on how their business was in comparisons to ours," he said lamely.

"Yeah, and lemme me find out you hitting some of the chicks in our club too. Old ass nigga, you need to keep your dick in your pants. And you over there buying white pussy and spending chips at the fuckin Gentlemen's Club. "

B.J. cleared his throat, looking uncomfortable and mumbled something unintelligible.

"Anyway, I'm in the process of making a move, a boss move. Lucky I'm a street nigga and know how to live off the fat of the land until this shit gets better."

"What you got in mind, young nigga?"

"I'ma make a few moves. We had some money saved up, and my shortie's college tuition, I'm about to invest it into a couple of bricks, bring in a million and weather this fuckin' storm."

B.J. put him on blast! "Young nigga have you lost your fuckin' mind! The only thing worse than an old fool is a young fool. Don't do it. Think about your family, it ain't worth it."

"Man, don't worry about me. Shit already in progress. Besides, Keisha is used to living a certain lifestyle, and she been with a nigga through thick in thin. We been having problems but we're working on it. After all she been through, she deserves this..."

Trigga's voice trailed off as he thought about the miscarriage. He'd been trying to build back their marriage to how it was sense then but there still was something amiss. There was unspoken tension in the air between them. Not to mention all this secretive shit Keisha was on. He needed to ask her about it. But did he really want to?

"I need to get this shit right for Keisha. She's always been with me... holdin' a nigga down," Trigga continued, seeing her in his mind's eye.

"Well, I don't know if she can wait for you through thick and thin in the federal pen," B.J. retorted with a snort.

"Nigga, I ain't going to the chain gang. Shit, I'd rather be carried by six than judged by twelve."

"That shit *sounds* slick. So what you saying is between dying and going to jail, either way, Keisha is going to wait?"

"Man, that ain't what I'm sayin'—"

"Well, what is you saying then? Y'all niggas got the game fucked up. A man's most prized possession is his family, his woman. You can't take a risk on that, and you damn sure can't lose your child's college fund and you and your woman's life savings, tryna fuckin' play street lottery for a quick fuckin' come up when the odds ain't in your favor."

For some reason, B.J. was fuming as he continued. "Because the truth is, you ain't living bad and a lot of niggas would love to be in your shoes. Don't throw it away over some fuckin' macho, hood rich bullshit," B.J. snapped, the cadence of his voice expanding as his eyes shot daggers at Trigga.

The moment lingered like thoughts at an impasse as the smoke from the blunt formed a halo over both their heads. The truth be told, the only reason Trigga had brought B.J. into the strip club business was that back in the day, B.J. used to own several strip clubs. Not just that, B.J. was once an infamous gangster who was feared by most and respected by all. As a child, Trigga had once watched B.J. walk up to Pookie Skeet, a rival drug dealer and shot him in the head point blank, range, BLOCKA! No questions, no talking, just one shot to the dome. Once Pookie Skeet's lifeless body hit the ground, the junkies ravaged the pockets of the dead man.

At the time, Trigga didn't know that it was all part of a tumultuous process that all young gangstas have to take, like some ghetto rite of passage in the ecology of the hood. Through B.J.'s reign of terror and bloodshed he was able to take over parts of New York's lucrative drug trade. He opened two very successful strip clubs, Dime Pieces and Cheetah's Club and restaurant. Then tragedy struck. The Feds came calling on a laundry list of charges.

Bryan Jackson, aka B.J., was indicted on conspiracy to traffic cocaine. He had no choice but to go to trial. At his trial, things only seemed to get worse. His best friend and his baby mama testified against him, each taking the stand in return for immunity against charges and $25,000 each. B.J. was convicted and sentenced to twenty years.

As fate would have it, when B.J. came home and was working a regular nine to five, Trigga gave him a job and was happy to do so. B.J.'s knowledge of running a strip club was incredible, except for one slight problem. B.J. couldn't keep his hands off the strippers.

Trigga grumbled his discontent as he rose from behind his desk to help gather up the nights' earnings and placed them in the safe. He had all of his earnings in from his business ventures, and money to be invested back into his grind.

"Man, I appreciate what you saying, and I know your knowledge ain't shit to be slept on. But for me, this is a crisis. Besides, I already paid for the dope, and Keisha ain't ever gone find out about it. She trusts a nigga one thousand, na'mean."

There was a soft rap at the door, causing B.J. and Trigga to exchange wary glances.

It was nearly five in the morning. The club was closed, and all of the employees should have been gone.

"Who is it?" Trigga raised his voice.

"It's me, Red," a tiny voice intoned.

"Fuck she still doing here?" Trigga scoffed as he tossed some money in the safe. B.J. gave him a shrug like, 'I don't know.'

"Come in!" Trigga said with annoyance.

Red walked in. She was a buxom woman, full figured, mostly bodacious ass and tits. Her body was covered with tattoos and body piercings. Her hair scarlet red. She had green cat like eyes, with high cheekbones that gave her a chic, Asian sex appeal. She wore a burgundy sarong with nothing under- neath; her ample breasts protruded with pink nipples the size of doorknobs.

"Fuck you still doin' here?" B.J. asked and stood. He frowned and winced as if he had a cramp in his leg.

"Shit, a bitch fell asleep in the back of the dressing room, and didn't nobody wake my ass up," she complained as her eyes swept over the room.

"That ain't my fucking job. Besides, if you got along with some of the other girls, maybe one of them would have woke you up," B.J. added.

"Humph, fuck dem hoes, they ain't got to like me, but they gonna respect me," Red sassed with a hand on her round hips, causing her gown to open, exposing more of her nude body. Even the small manicured patch of her vagina was red and shaped like a heart.

The truth was, Red was one of the baddest chicks in the club, and she knew it. She was one of the top three earners. However, she had one major setback, she was a self-centered egotistical backstabbing bitch. So much so, that she had refused to socialize with all the other girls in the club, even the ones who tried to befriend her.

The rapper known as Fabolous used to frequent the club just to holla at a bodaciously sexy stripper by the name of Melody. She was from the Bronx. Melody just happened to be a redbone like Red; only she was thicker in all the right places. She was also younger with a face of an angel. Red envied the stripper so much that she told one of Fabolous' homies that Melody had AIDS, and a bad case of herpes. Ironically, Melody found out that Red had lied on her out of jealousy, and the two women nearly went to blows in the dressing room one day.

After the incident, the rest of the girls stopped associating with her. On more than several occasions she'd violated the club's most disciplined rule, and that was, not to date any of the clubs patrons. Not only did she date the patrons, but she also sold sex to many of the baller and dope boy patrons boldly in the club, and had been caught twice by B.J. having sex in the private dance booths. She should have been fired immediately, but for some reason, B.J. let her keep her job. Trigga had his suspicions about why.

"Fuck you want, Red?" Trigga asked, suppressing a yawn as he glanced at his wrist for the third time. He was getting sleepy.

"Let a bitch outta here. The fuckin' door is locked, and I need to be getting my beauty rest," she said in a sing song voice with the animation of a sex kitten as she crossed her arms over her bosom and leaned against the door frame, thrusting her large double D breasts forward.

"Naw, what you need to be doing is stop turning my club into a whore house and fucking niggas, then maybe your ass wouldn't be so damn tired and falling asleep on the job."

Red's mouth formed a big incredulous O as she gasped, face flushed red. She cut her eyes at B.J., optic slants of disdain.

"Who told you some shit like that?!" She huffed as she snaked her neck.

"B.J. did, and it has happened on several occasions. You really trying me now with this," Trigga snapped.

Red sprang off the doorframe and was in B.J.'s face confrantional.

"Oh, B.J., really? Well, did he tell you he asked me to suck his dick for a hundred dollars, and said he wouldn't tell? Huh, did you tell him that, bitch?!"

"Stop lying, gurl," B.J. persuaded by placing a hand on her shoulder and nudging her toward the door.

"Oh, and I'm lying?!" She shoved him away from her and balled up her tiny fist as if she was about to strike him.

"Right, and Trigga don't have time to hear your bullshit," B.J. said with a nervous edge to his voice. "Gone girl."

"Yes, I do because if it's true, I'll fire both of y'all asses."

Trigga's harsh words got their attention. B.J. shot Red an apologetic plea as he said barely above a whisper, "Come on now, Red, don't cause no problems in here. Now stop with the foolishness." By then, B.J. was damn near wrestling with her to get her out the door.

"Humph, you fuckin' started it with that fuckin' dry snitch shit, tellin' him I'm selling pussy—"

B.J. shoved her so hard toward the door that her neck snapped back and her wig fell over her face as her feet left scuff marks on the carpet.

"We good, boss. It was just a little misunderstanding" B.J. grinned like the Cheshire cat that had got caught swallowing the bird whole, feathers and all. Leaving out, he continued to shove Red out the door, but still her voice could be heard echoing down the long hallway.

"Stop, get your damn hands off me..."

After they were gone, Trigga couldn't help but chuckle to himself. He knew that B.J. had been making sexual advances toward the girls because they told on him. Truth be told, he couldn't blame B.J. After spending all that time in prison, then to come home, working at Lair was like working with a harem full of beautiful, exotic women.

As soon as Trigga had placed the last stack of money in the safe, B.J. returned. He was winded, his shirt was soiled with perspiration stains under each arm, and there was a scratch on his hand with blood.

"Man, don't be believing shit dat bitch sayin'. She just mad 'cause I be doin' my job."

"Yeah, whatever, B.J., but don't let one of them get you tricked out your job—"

Trigga was just about to say more when the office door burst open and three masked gunmen rushed in. Trigga reached for his banger.

Blocka! Blocka! BANG! BANG!

A fulisade of shots rang out!

Vaguely, Trigga could hear B.J. yell out in agony as he fell to the floor. He was shot several times, his body riddled with bullets.

Trigga had been caught slipping in the worst way.

---

7

*T*he impact of the first bullet nearly toppled Trigga as it propelled him backward over the chair; the second bullet grazed his skull. The .9mm he was reaching for was dislodged from his hand, and it careened across the carpet out of reach.

"Get your muthafuckin' hands where I can see 'em, fuck nigga!" a raspy voice barked as two assailants raced around Trigga's desk gathering up money.

Trigga had been shot several times. Once in the shoulder and arm, and a bullet grazed his skull. B.J. had been hit in the chest, in his abdomen, and neck, and at least three times in parts of his lower extremities and was badly leaking blood.

In all the chaos, Trigga lay on his back dazed, with the ceiling spinning. He could hear the grisly sound of B.J. struggling to breathe. He was gurgling, gasping a horrid noise as blood spewed from his mouth and nose. The gaping hole in his neck gushed blood like a faucet turned on high.

Somebody was riffling through Trigga's pockets. His thick diamond and gold chain was snatched off his neck. One of the masked gunmen stood over him, intimidating like death in the flesh. Trigga could see the white of his fiendish eyes and a big bulbous nose through the ski mask. He could also make out what looked like a sinister gloating grin, as if the gunman was enjoying this moment.

"Fuck nigga, we meet again." The voice sounded familiar as Trigga lay in the puddle of crimson blood that was starting to form underneath him.

Trigga couldn't answer if he wanted to. His mind was in a daze as the room continued to spin out of control like he was on a Ferris wheel, and the solitary light bulb overhead was suddenly a bright light strobing his mind like a morning sun.

"It's only about three hundred grand here," a voice intoned. It belonged to one of the gunmen.

The gunman who had been standing over him, violently snatched up Trigga by his collar. His face was only inches away from Trigga's when he spoke with grit in his voice, spraying Trigga's face with spittle and deadly intent.

"Where the rest of the money at, fuck nigga. And where that dope too?" The gunman asked with a firm grip on Trigga's collar.

No answer.

The masked assailant reached back and began to punch Trigga repeatedly in his face.

"Talk! Where the fuckin' money and dope at, nigga?!"

Blood dripped from Trigga's mouth. He was semi-conscious, and his face was a bloody pulp of a mess.

"That's it... no mo' money... no dope..." Trigga groaned painfully.

WHAM!

He was violently struck again. The gun was placed to the side of his head.

"Okay, here is the deal, pussy ass nigga. I need two million dollars, just like you took from me, and I need it within two weeks, or I'm going to hurt what you love most. Now try me, nigga! You lucky I let your bitch ass live."

Suddenly Trigga felt the hand around his neck began to choke him.

"You hear me, nigga!?" the voice asked.

From somewhere in the deep crevices of Trigga's mind, he tried to place where he knew the voice from.

All Trigga could do was croak a weak, "Yes," as he gasped for air and blood dripped from his face.

"By next Friday, nigga. If I don't get my money by then, I'ma handle my business. I want you to deliver the money to a location. You will hear from me by then. Understand, you will be hearing from me soon. Real talk, fuck boy!"

"Yes..."

WHAM!

Trigga was struck again. He feigned to be knocked out, but he could hear the gunman moving around, scurrying about as footfalls moved past his head.

Then, he heard one of the gunmen whisper, "Dat bitch said it would be more money than this."

Another gunman commented, "Fuck dat. This is still a good lick. Let's bounce!"

They continued to ransack his office, then, just as quickly as they had come, they left like a violent tornado leaving destruction in their wake.

TRIGGA LAY PERFECTLY STILL on the mauve carpet, saturating the pale surface with his blood as the rancid stench of gun smoke and blood permeated his nostrils. His pounding heartbeat throbbed in his throat.

From somewhere in the quietness, the hum of death beckoned. Trigga heard a horrific gurgling sound and coughing. He craned his neck to look, and to his dismay, B.J. was seated with his back against the file cabinet as he clutched his throat, eyes big as saucers as blood ran from his neck like a spigot. His eyes were spread wide with fear, as if he was going into shock or worse.

"We... ain't gon'... make it, man..." Fingers like claws clasped at his throat as he tried to stop the bleeding, to stop the death, his own demise.

"Yes, we is, B.J.... you a fighter, man...we good," Trigga managed to say, but in his heart, he was prepared for the inevitable as he patted his pockets in search of something.

Trigga fished in his pocket for his iPhone and managed to dial 911. He gave the operator his location, and as the operator continued to talk, he disconnected the call and dialed Keisha. His last call.

She answered on the second ring with a groggy voice, like she was barely awake.

"Hey, bae, when you coming home? I was having these nightmares—"

"Keesh, baby, I love you... I've been shot. It's kinda bad, B.J. too..."

"WHAAT!?" she screamed into the phone so loud that she woke Cam. He had crawled into the bed in the wee hours of the night without her knowing it.

"... but I'ma be all right. I just want you and Cam to know I love you..."

Before he could finish his sentence, Keisha had jumped out the bed and had her robe on and house shoes. She began to pull on Cam to wake him up.

"Did you call an ambulance? Where you at? I'm on my way, baby, hang in there. I love you too, please don't die on me!"

Her poignant words segued into sobs, as she minced each one like plaintive pleas. She was talking a mile a minute and moving faster as she listened for a response.

To hear his voice.

To know he was okay.

Was he still alive?

Silence hummed.

There was no response on the other end of the phone.

Keisha completely lost it!!

"TRIGGA!? TRIGGA?! Answer this fuckin' phone. Trigga, you hear me?!" Keisha screamed.

With enormous strength she didn't even know she had, she picked Cam up off the bed with one hand, carried him out the door in his pajamas, and got into her car, then headed straight for Trigga's club. The entire time, Keisha couldn't remember ever praying so hard in her life. She prayed for Trigga not to die on her and Cam.

She prayed for him to be alive, but in her heart, she knew there was a chance this time that God might not answer her prayer.

KEISHA PULLED up to Trigga's club in her white 750 BMW. The streets were cluttered with fire trucks, ambulances and police cars galore with their ardent lights stabbing away at the ominous gray swarthy night. The luminous full moon sat high in the fuchsia colored sky with a hint of dawn about to peek down from the heavens.

Keisha hopped out the car, not even caring that she was dressed slovenly in her housecoat and slippers, nude underneath except for panties, no bra. As she prepared to cross the street, she ducked under the yellow crime scene tape. She was accosted by a large burly white cop, just as a gurney rushed by carrying a body with a sheet covering it. For a fleeting second, she looked at it then tore her eyes away as they filled with tears. It couldn't be him.

"Hey! Where you think you're going?" the burly cop asked brusquely and pushed his enormous girth in front her, blocking her path.

"That's my husband inside there. This is our club."

"You can't go inside! It's a crime scene." He shoved her and she shoved back.

Losing her patience, Keisha hollered as she tried to push by the huge cop.

"You're not listening to me. This is my fucking club, my husband is inside. I need to know if he is okay. I need to see him. I need to be with him."

Her poignant words fell on deaf ears. "First off, I have strict orders not to let anyone inside until the investigation is over. And second, ma'am, if that was your husband inside, I think you need to talk to the medical examiner or the priest. This scene has been label a homicide investigation. You're going to have to leave now. Or I'm going—"

"Homicide investigation?"

"Yes, your husband is dead."

With the cop's last words, Keisha dropped to her knees and began to wail pitifully with her forehead against the cold concrete. Prostrating like a Muslim in prayer.

"NOOOOOOO. NOOOO, God NOOOOOO," she wailed and began to pound her fist on the worn pavement until she felt hands on her shoulders. She pulled away and looked up through teary eyes, only to see Cam. His starry eyes were misty with tears threatening burst.

"Mommy, don't cry. Where is Daddy at?" he asked innocently.

She pulled her chin up high and just looked at her son, the spitting image of his dad. Cam was barefoot except for his red Spiderman socks. She swallowed the dry lump in her throat and spoke with a trembling tune.

"Baby.... your daddy... your daddy... oh, God..." She stammered and broke down, holding him in her arms and rocking him steady, as if it was just him and her in the world.

"Ma'am, I'm not going to ask you again. You're going to have to move off the premises," the cop stoically said as feet and phantom figures moved around, urgently shuffling by in lurid night lights.

Something deep within her exploded, and Keisha sprang to her feet with the quickness. Her fist was in his face, like she was about to strike the cop. Keisha was about to lose the little bit of sanity that she had been desperately trying to cling to.

She was livid! "Fuck you mean get off the premises? I own the fucking premises, and my god damn husband is in there, a-fuckin'-alive."

She yelled so loud, cops and paramedics walking by stopped what they were doing.

"Mommy, no, don't fight him," Cam said, tugging on her housecoat sleeve. She looked down and discovered her robe was was open, and all her nudity exposed. There was a light chill in the air. She fastened the thin sheer material and sucked in a deep breath of frustration, ignoring the people gawking at her. Then, from a distance, she heard a loud metal clang, and a door squeaked open. People, mostly emergency medics and police, gathered around as the gurney with the body was lifted onto the ambulance. Something drastic occurred to her.

"TRIGGA!" she screamed at the top of her lungs and took off into a sprint, gown flowing in the wind, breast exposed in the night-chilled air.

She shoved several medics away and grabbed the steel metal gurney with tears streaming down her cheeks. In an instant, she felt hands pulling on her, tugging her as they admonished her.

"Stop!"

"What is she doing?" the medics said in chorus.

She pulled away. "If this is my husband, I need to see him, I need to know." She pushed forward again and grabbed at the white sheet, then pulled away. There was a ripple of hushed drones, and a long, protracted wail that sounded like a wounded animal in agony, something ungodly.

It was Keisha, she had completely lost it. She was overwhelmed with shock and despair.

8

The burly cop who had confronted her earlier rushed up again. He was winded like he had just run a marathon. His pasty white skin was flushed pale, his brow was creased with angry, indignant lines as he grabbed Keisha by her wrist and attempted to place a handcuff on it. She pulled away and kicked him. The medics scattered like the devil was on the loose.

"Get your fuckin' hands off me!" Keisha kicked again, barely missing the officer's testicles.

Several other officers rushed up and grabbed her. Her arms were violently placed behind her back, her ample breasts fully exposed. Her son rushed over to protect his mother.

"Leave my mama alone!" Cam cried out. A cop scooped Cam high as he thrashed.

"Put my fuckin' child down," Keisha managed to say as she was being manhandled by cops.

"Yo! Yo! Y'all get yo' fuckin' dick beaters off my wife and child. Fuck wrong wit'cha!?"

The crude voice belonged to Trigga, and he was thirty-eight hot! He was shirtless with bloody bandages wrapped around his head, chest, and arm. It looked like he had been dipped in blood upside down. He could barely walk as he was being escorted by two black homicide detectives and a female medic, who had been trying to get him on a stretcher, or a wheelchair. He stubbornly refused, and it was obvious by looking at his bullet-riddled body covered in blood, that he was lucky to be alive and in bad condition.

"You know her?" one of the detectives wearing an expensive two-piece gray suit with shiny gray Stacy Adams shoes and a matching wide brim fedora hat asked as his partner looked on with a writing pen poised in his hand, as if he were taking notes as other cops rushed by.

"That's my fuckin' wife and son," Trigga shouted angrily and grimaced in pain as blue and red lights strobed his features in the gruesome dim of the night.

"Do you think she can help us come up with any info concerning what happened?" one of the cops asked.

Trigga looked at him like he was crazy! "Man, fuck outta here. Naw, muthafucka, and take them goddamn cuffs off her and stop with the rough-neck shit on her and my kid," Trigga raged and attempted to rush over.

The cop with the wide brim hat stalled him with the help of his partner and a medic.

Things were about to get bad.

The homicide detective with the wide brim hat spoke with authority.

"Hey! Bruce, don't handcuff her. She is one of the victims' wife, and that's his kid." His partner walked over to ease the situation that was sure to get volatile at any minute.

Too late!

"You punk ass muthafuckin' pussy ass pigs. Get your damn hand off me!" Keisha said as soon as the cuffs were off.

"I didn't know who she was, coming up in here wild-eyed, acting like she was on drugs—" the burly cop was about to say with his hands raised apologetically.

"You telling a muthafuckin' lie, BITCH! I told you I was his wife!" Keisha shouted, then rushed over to Trigga and jumped into his arms. He cried out in pain, and the two of them nearly toppled over and fell. Others had to grab them.

"Ouch, shit!"

"I'm sorry, baby. I thought you was dead. I thought they had killed you. When I looked under that sheet and saw that it was B.J. and not you, I lost it," she sobbed, pecking his face with kisses as the baby Cam meandered over and hugged his dad's pants leg. Trigga was able to caress his son's head.

From the outside looking in, the horrific scene was pathetic as the three of them huddled, engulfed in ambient blue and red emergency lights flashing in the murky night with Trigga covered from head to toe in blood.

Then the inevitable happened. It was a miracle that Trigga was even able to walk, considering the severity of his wounds and the amount of blood he was losing. All of a sudden, Trigga collapsed. He would have fallen on his face if not for Keisha and the detectives grabbing him in the nick of time.

TRIGGA LAY in bed with tubes in his nose, and an I.V. bottle was connected to his arm. The episodic beeps chimed rhythmically in perfect sequence with his pounding heartbeat, as if serenading his will to survive. In the distance, a television blared a Ninja Turtles cartoon as Cam sat at the foot of the bed, legs dangling, fascinated with his favorite cartoon show.

Sitting in a chair next to Trigga was Keisha. Oblivious, she pecked away at her phone while occasionally laughing at some of the antics on her Face-book and Instagram page with friends as she chatted, ambidextrous fingers deftly pecking away in a blur. Then her face changed when the phone began to vibrate. Picking up the call, she walked out of the room to speak but Trigga was able to pick up on a few words as she paced in front of the door.

"I can't come right now but I'll come see you as soon as I can...Yes...I'm excited. I—I can't wait. See you soon."

She ended the call as Trigga lay still in the bed, unmoving and wondering who it was his wife was so eager to see. Walking in, Keisha sat down in her place next to his bed and continued pecking away on her phone.

Trigga stirred and slightly moved his neck, turning in her direction and looking at her. She hadn't noticed as she continued to poke away at her screen, laughng, and giggling with her friends, at a meme. Something about Chris Brown feuding with his baby mama.

"Dadddy!!" Cam squealed with delight. He hopped from the bed with agility and rushed to his bedside.

"Heyy, lil man... you need a haircut." Trigga ruffled his son's hair. They shared a laugh as Cam hugged him.

Smiling dreamily, Keisha just stared. Father and son. This was a picture perfect moment.

The two of them are inseparable. For some strange reason, Keisha felt a pang of jealousy. She cleared her throat, a rude gesture to get both of their attention.

"Uh, hello."

"Uh, hello what? You over there as usual pounding away on that damn phone, probably on Facebook or one of your social media sites."

"For your information, I was not. I was looking at some houses," she lied with a grin and they both knew it.

"Yeah, right," Trigga commented facetiously and made a comical face at her.

Keisha couldn't help but laugh out loud.

"Okay, I was looking at some houses earlier, and I just happened to check out my page. I was bored, baby."

Together, the two of them burst out in giddy laughter as Keisha got up and sat on the bed with them. Cutting his eyes at Cam who was looking back at the television, Trigga decided to ask her about the call she'd taken in the hall.

"Who was that you were on the phone with?" he inquired, dropping his voice so that only she could hear.

Keisha's brows rose in surprise, her mouth forming into an o-shape as her pupils danced back and forth but never met his eyes. She was working up a lie and Trigga knew it. Suspicion began to curve his mouth as he watched her stammer out her words.

"I—It's just something I'm working on. Some business stuff...don't worry about it right now," Keisha assured him, painfully aware of how stilted her voice sounded. She placed her hand on his chest and he closed his eyes, enjoying the feel of her touch against his skin. There was no reason to be question Keisha. She was the love of his life and whatever reason she had for holding in information was for his own good. Had to be. But still Trigga couldn't ignore the unpleasant twist in his stomach telling him something was wrong.

Affectionately, she kissed Trigga's cheek above the large gauze that was tinged red, quieting his worries and instantly sending him into a lustful state. He tried to palm her butt, but she swatted his hand away.

"Stop. Not in front of him," she giggled, pointing towards Cameron who had now rotated around, his eyes fixed on his parents.

"Daddy, when you coming home?" Cameron asked with a child's pouting lips.

"I dunno, Cam. I hope soon," Trigga responded and looked at Keisha.

In the background, a public announcement system blared. Then, suddenly, Trigga remembered something. He craned his neck and writhed in pain. His words were slow and lethargic, like his tongue had weight on it.

"How long have I been here, and what happened to B.J.? Is he okay?"

Keisha turned her head. She didn't want him to see the stricken look on her face. Trigga squeezed, her hand.

"KEISHA!" He called her name in a halting deep baritone, causing her to flinch.

She turned to him with her bottom lip trembling, heart beating fast. In so many ways, B.J. was like the father he never had, a mentor he could listen to. His childhood hero, a hood gangsta.

"Baby... he didn't make it. He's dead." She could feel her body trembling, heart quaking as a gale of emotions consumed her.

She continued, "I'm sorry. I know that was your dude. You liked him a lot, baby."

She noticed when his entire body went rigid, his mighty hands gripped at the white sheets so hard she heard his knuckles crack. He bristled in anger and Keisha could feel the heat of his fury as it radiated from off of him. But then comes the sorrow. Trigga closed his eyes and turned away from her, facing the gray barren wall next to the window. She saw a lone tear cascade down his bronze chin before he quickly mopped at it with the back of his hand. She played it off like she didn't see it.

"Cam, baby, let Mommy and Daddy talk for a moment alone. Go sit on the chair over there."

"Okay, Mommy," he said jovially and walked to the chair.

Trigga continued to stare at the wall with his brow furrowed, not blinking, not moving. Just subdued by his thoughts. Then, suddenly, he asked. "How long have I been here?"

His voice was hoarse, but forceful. He opened his eyes. His brow was creased with apprehension and something else that Keisha couldn't discern. Fear?

"You have been here three days,"

"B.J. is dead." He repeated out of nowhere, as if he was trying to find solace in his friend's death.

"Bae, I am so sorry."

His body stiffened. A sibilant sigh escaped his bruised lips. There was a partial purple and black ring under his right eye, and a lump almost the size of a golf ball in his forehead. He muttered something unintelligible. She squeezed his hand and wished she could take his pain away, take the moment away, but they are both trapped, held hostage in the turbulent moment, a tidal wave of raw emotions that threatened to consume them.

Keisha tried to ignore Cam sitting in the chair with his legs dangling, hands crossed in his lap, watching them intensely.

"When I arrived at the club, I saw them placing a body in the ambulance..." Her voice cracked with emotion. "I thought it was you under the sheet." She nibbled on her lip, trying not to regurgitate the bad memories, like the nightmare she was having the moment Trigga had called and told her he had been shot, again.

"What about B.J.'s funeral and the club?" Trigga asked. His voice was husky, dry like sandpaper dragged across concrete.

"I paid for the funeral. As for the club, I've been running it with the help of Yadi. She's handling everything there while I take care of the administrative—"

"You fuckin' whaat!?" Trigga snapped.

"I paid for the funeral."

"I'm not talkin' 'bout no fuckin' funeral. What the hell you doin' runnin' the club? It's dangerous. I almost got murdered in there and my nigga B.J. was killed. Are you fuckin' crazy? And Yadi, she would steal me blind!"

"No, are you crazy yelling at me and cursing n' shit in front of Cam like you lost your damn mind, nigga?" Keisha hissed between clenched teeth, barely above a whisper, with eyes ablaze.

It took everything in Trigga to bridle his anger. The reality was he could never beat Keisha in arguing, and to attempt such a feat in his fragile condition would be futile at best. So, he tried a different approach, a better tactic. He attempted diplomacy and lowered his voice.

"Keesh, come on, man. Fuck you doin'? You can't be working at the club, especially after what happened to me. You lost your fuckin' mind." As hard as he tried, the wrong words just slipped out his mouth like water seeping through a cracked dam about to burst. And as he expected, it burst alright. Keisha went in on him.

"Have you lost your mind, Trigga? WE got bills to pay, WE got car notes to pay, house notes, daycare to pay—"

Trigga held up a hand to declare a truce.

"Alright, alright, I got it!"

"No you don't got it. If your ass ends up dead, no disrespect, but me and my baby gotta eat, we gotta survive. Besides, you not telling me what the hell is going on. I looked in the stash spot in the safe in the attic, and the money was gone. Cam's college money and our life savings are gone. What did you do with it? What are you hiding from me?"

Shit, she found out about the money. Think fast, think fast, his mind churned.

9

"It's in a safe place." he lied. For some reason, quite possibly the narrowed look of suspicion on Keisha's face, he felt his heartbeat faster.

"Why did you move it? It was already in a safe place. Supposed something would have happened to you?" she asked.

"I invested it into stocks and bonds, trying to get our chips for that new house you want, bae," Trigga countered, giving her a tilted smile that he hoped would ease the tension around them.

"Uhh, uhh," Keisha grumbled like she wasn't buying his story one bit. And she wasn't. But she had her own secrets that she kept in for his sake and decided to put her faith in him that he was doing the same.

Trigga quickly changed the subject.

"Have the police come up with anything?" he asked and shifted in his bed like it was uncomfortable.

"Yes."

"Who?"

"You."

"Me?"

"Well...they are kinda investigating you."

"Wha-da-fuck!"

"Stop cursing!"

"Man, shit! How am I supposed to be a suspect? I got shot, and my dude was killed," Trigga said, shaking his head. He raised his head off the pillow and looked her in disbelief, then continued angrily. "I'm the nigga that got shot, my dude got murked, and I'm a suspect. Come on man. This like déjà vu all over again!" He whined in that nasal tone that always seemed to get under her skin when they were having a contentious exchange of words.

It *was* like déjà vu. She knew what he was referring to. The very night they'd met he'd got shot and woke up to police questioning him for being a suspect in a crime. And here he was again.

"Yep, 'cause you got a track record, been a suspect in over a half dozen homicides, and they found a gun. They're checking it for ballistics. If it matches the gun that B.J. was killed with or any other homicides, they threatened to charge you with murder. We have been through this before, you know the drill, and I'm getting sick of it. Like, you ain't gon' never change!"

"Fuck outta here. What I look like killing B.J.? And it's not my fault some niggas ran up in my spot. And what the hell you talking about you getting sick of ?" Trigga quipped, incensed as he tilted his head to the side. "You don't have to worry about shit. I'm the one who takes care of everything so that you don't have to. What the hell can you be sick of?"

"Stop cursing, nigga! And I know you didn't do it, but it's like trouble seems to follow you. It was just a few years ago that you were in this same exact situation, shot up in the hospital about to catch a case with the law. Trigga, I love you, but I can't keep doing this. We have a child now."

Trigga mopped his face with weary hands and almost knocked over the IV stand. Keisha had to catch it from toppling over.

"Sounds like you ready to bail on a nigga," Trigga blurted out followed by an exasperated sigh.

Keisha softened her tone. "Bae, I'm not saying that, but something ain't right. All our money is gone, and I feel like you're lying to me. And that bobble headed chick at the club keeps asking about you more than the other females. I mean, I know you're her boss, but damn!" Keisha said, making a face.

"Which one?"

"Red. That chick that everybody hate."

"Red??"

Suddenly, Trigga remembered something and sat up in bed, causing excruciating pain to ricochet throughout his body.

Instantly, his mind had a murky flashback, and he remembered what happened on that dark and dreary day. Suspiciously, Red came to the office late. They were counting up the night's receipts. She peeped the open safe. And the money. Moments after she left, the masked gunmen stormed his office with guns blazing.

She set them up. Trigga made an oath in his mind to kill her, to avenge what she did.

"Fuckin' bitch!" Trigga hissed under his breath through a tight jaw. Looking at Keisha who was staring at him intently, he pinched his lips together and gave her a look she knew all too well.

"Trigga, I ain't stupid. It's something going on. You need to tell me something!"

But she knew it was no use. Mums the word, real killers move in silence. Trigga always tried to keep Keisha out of his drama, thus not making her an accessory to murder. There was no doubt in his mind he was going to kill Red with his bare hands. Then something occurred to him.

"Fuck, what is today?" he asked, raising up to a seated position as he searched the room for anything that would tell him the date.

"Wednesday," Keisha replied.

"Wednesday?! Oh, God. I gotta get out of here," was all Trigga said. He had forgotten all about the threat the gunman made if he didn't have the money by next Friday. He'd wasted too much time already.

"Trigga, you ain't going nowhere in your condition!" Keisha admonished, jumping up to stop him.

"Shit, I'm leavin' outta here. I'm outta dis bitch."

Trigga got up from the bed, and Keisha grabbed his arm.

"You not going nowhere like this!" Keisha shouted.

"You don't understand. I got to GO!" He retorted as his eyes frantically looked around the room.

"Mama, Daddy, don't fight," Cam said in a voice filled with melancholy.

They ignored him. They were both caught up in the riotous storm of emotions, with Trigga being more determined than either of them would ever know.

With one last effort, Keisha was determined to talk some sense into his stubborn brain. She pulled his arm, and he snatched away causing the I.V.'s intravenous needle to pull out of his arm.

Keisha spoke as if she was prepared for this very moment, this very confrontation, as she stated firmly, "TRIGGA, so help me God, if you leave out this hospital its over between us!" She spoke firmly with an attitude as he walked up close on him, but she wasn't prepared for his quick response.

"I'd rather it be over between the two of us, than seeing you dead in a casket!" Touché!

Keisha snapped her neck back like she had been punched in the face, and watched in horror as Trigga began to painstakingly gather his meager gear, clothes that she had brought him for when it was time for him to leave.

"So you leaving, huh?" she asked curtly, with her head cocked at an angle.

"I have till next Friday to figure out some shit, and time ain't on my side," Trigga responded while putting on his shoes.

"I hope it has nothing to do with that stupid ass note about giving somebody 2 million dollars that I found on the door because if it is, and you're not telling me, I'm going to be mad as hell, " she said.

Trigga looked up at her, thoughts percolating, just as a doctor walked in, bringing with him the murmur of hospital noises. In his hand was a clipboard and some type of surgical instrument. A tuft of gray hair ringed his head. The top of his pate was going bald. The doctor did a second take with a raised brow over his half spec bifocals. Trigga was fully dressed.

"Your injuries are not life threatening, but you need time to hea—"

Trigga stood while the doctor was talking and brushed by him and stalked over to where his son lay asleep. He gently bent down and kissed him on the cheek.

"I love you lil, nigga," he whispered and turned to look at Keisha.

"Humph!" She huffed with her face balled up and placed her arms over her chest.

Trigga walked out the door with the doctor staring back and forth between the both of them.

"TRIGGGA!!"

10

Trigga rode to his club in the back of an Uber cab. The bright city lights looked ominous and grim to him for some reason. Probably because death was on his mind. The ride was so bumpy it felt like he was going to injure himself, but that was something he would just have to deal with. He couldn't wait to get back to the club and find the stripper Red, he thought as he pulled out his phone to look her up on social media.

He found her page on Facebook. There she was in all her glory, dressed in a two-piece sequin gold bathing suit that highlighted the tats decorating her body. Behind her was a pile of money, big face hundreds. Lots of money. His money, he imagined.

"The fuckin' bitch!" he said aloud and smacked the glass window with the palm of his hand. The sound resonated like a gunshot in the small confines of the cab. The Indian cab driver jumped in his seat and peered with suspicion in the review mirror at Trigga. The cab driver then dug under his seat in search something, a weapon. He found it and pulled it out. It was a miniature baseball bat.

"Aye, you got problem?" he yelled at Trigga through the thick plastic window. His English was terrible.

"Yeah, your Arab ass taking too long in this raggedy ass cab."

Trigga couldn't get to the club fast enough. Suddenly his phone chimed. He peeped the number. He could barely contain his joy despite his circumstances. It's Keisha, she is longing for his touch already, in need of his love. Despite the perils of the moment, he felt genuinely touched.

"Hey, bae." He beamed into the phone as a smiled pulled at his lips. He noticed the cab driver watching him intensely in the mirror just as Keisha began to blast him. Not at all what he was expecting.

"Nigga don't 'hey bae' me! Right now as we speak, I'm packin' up all your shit and preparing to have a yard sale, clothes, video games, and all, nigga. What I don't sell, I'm giving to my Uncle Pookie who just came home from the Fed... Nigga, done tried me with that bullshit," she muttered under her breath as if talking to herself.

Trigga took his ear away from the phone and looked at it, perplexed, just as another call came in. He recognized the number instantly. It was Queen. He quickly switched over as Keisha continued ranting.

"What's good?" He tried to sound jovial, unperturbed. In his old line of business, and especially where he came from, it wasn't good to get shot up all the time. To date, Trigga has had more stitches than a used king size mattress from all the shootouts and fist fights he had been in.

"I heard you got hit up again...bad," Queen said. Trigga could hear some type of music in the background. Club music.

"How you know about that?" he asked, picking up on some voices in the background.

Queen didn't answer and he knew she wouldn't. She probably considered it to be a rhetorical question being that she made it a habit to answer to no one. Picking up on the noise behind her, he could've sworn he heard someone ask her if she wanted a drink. Odd. Queen didn't seem like the clubbing type.

"It is what it is," Trigga continued. "I'm good, now. A nigga on gorilla mode now, 'bout to go on a search and destroy mission."

"What happened?" she asked.

"Niggas hit up my club. Caught me slippin' and slumped one of my dudes, my O.G. I'm hot 'bout dat shit, na'mean."

"Yeah, that's unfortunate," she replied without emotion. "How you feeling? Let me know if it's anything I can do. Anything you need."

"Okay, right now, I'm just trying to put this shit together."

"Put what together?" Queen asked. Trigga pondered if he should tell her that somebody was trying to press him for two million dollars; an old school extortion game. He decided against telling her because only peons get extorted, and ninety percent of the time, it's a gangsta doing the extortion.

Trigga felt he was the ultimate gangsta, so he decided to keep his mouth shut.

Gangstas don't pay extortion, his mind churned.

"I just need to time to put shit together... Ouch!" he complained in pain. The cab driver had run over a pothole the size of a small city, it felt like.

"Man, watch them big ass holes."

"Fuuck you!" The cab driver shot back, waving the small baseball bat. Sneering at him, Trigga turned back to his call.

"As I was saying, I need to get my shit together, beef up security at my spot. You know, basic shit. Anyway, what's up with you? I know you ain't call to shoot the breeze with a nigga." The cab driver ran over another pothole. Trigga slapped the plastic window as he grimaced in pain.

"Nothing, just checking in on you. You know you my boy," she responded. The words didn't even sound right rolling off Queen's lips. She wasn't one for small talk. She wanted something.

"Queen, I know you better than that. What's really good?" he drawled comically in a monotone.

Queen couldn't help but laugh. "Okay, Trigga, you know me well. The reason I am calling you is I need someone for a caper—"

"Queen, you know I'm retired now, doing the family shit. I promised Keisha I wouldn't—"

"It pays five mill," she interjected.

"Five mill? Damn, they must want a nigga to kill Obama or some shit."

"No, but close. It's a Federal witness. A guy name Willie Vasquez."

"Kingpin, Willie Vasquez! The muthafuckin' billionaire ass Mexican baron."

Queen chuckled. "Make that kingpin turned snitch. He has a ten million dollar bounty out on his head, dead or alive."

"Man, I'm stayin' away from that shit. Dem muthafuckin' Mexicans some crazy ass niggas. But hold up, if the job pays five mill and the bounty is ten million, I'm not a mathematician, but it's five million lost some were in the sauce, feel me?"

"Naw, your ass worried about the wrong thing. You get five mill, take it or leave it."

Trigga contemplated what she said. He could use the money, but he didn't have time for some dare devil 'kill a Mexican' shit.

"I'ma have to pass on this one. You know I would do it but Keesh and I are already going through enough shit and she'd kill me if I went back to that life. But thanks, Queen, a nigga forever in your debt."

"Okay, but you missing out on a good lick. It's an inside job, we actually have a Federal agent that is part of the witness protection plan helping us."

Trigga was tempted, knowing that it was an inside job always helped, but he stood his ground.

"Naw, I'ma have to pass on this one, but thanks... Oh, shit, I forgot I have Keisha on the other end. Bye!" Trigga switched back over to Keisha. She was still yelling into the phone, completely oblivious to the fact that he had been gone.

"...and I will change the muthafuckin' locks! I'm sick of your shit, and I want my fuckin' money, punk ass nigga, and I am getting a court order to get full custody of our child—"

Trigga interrupted. "Keesh, stop it, man. I have not stolen no money. You think I would do that?"

"What's wrong? Something you not telling me? Talk to me!" she yelled into the phone.

"It's nothing," he said in an attempt to brush her off.

"You said you wouldn't lie to me. You said we wouldn't keep secrets from each other. Talk to me. Tell me what's going on. I'm your ride or die with marriage paperwork and all. But if you keep lying, I'm about to end all of that."

"I'm not keeping a secret," he told her.

Then Trigga's resolved shattered, and with a deep sigh, he tried a different approach.

"If I tell you, you're not going to trip and think I'm crazy again."

"No, I am not. Just don't say no stupid shit cause I'm this close to canceling the yard sale and just throwing bleach all over your shit and giving your games to them homeless people on 47th street."

"Okay, I really do feel like that was Lloyd that I saw at the club, and—"

CLICK!

"Keisha! Keisha!" Trigga looked at the phone and cursed. "Bitch hung up on me." He kicked the seat in back of the cab driver.

"Wut' chu do dat fo?" the angry cab driver asked with his eyes flaming red.

He swerved the cab to the side of the street and barely missed getting hit by a school bus when he hopped out and slung upon the back door where Trigga was seated, catching him completely by surprise. That wasn't all that caught him by surprise.

"Nigger no can ride in cab no more!" That was the first time the Indian cab driver had pronounced anything right.

Fuming mad, Trigga hopped out the cab on a busy intersection.

"Fuck you just call me?!" Trigga was prepared to swing on the cab driver until he saw he was armed with a miniature bat, full intending to hit Trigga with it. He could tell by the malicious intent in the man's eyes.

"Yu no in condition to fight. I beat ass," he said looking at Trigga's arm in the sling, and reached back like he was going to strike Trigga, causing him to duck and take a step back. That was when the cab driver seized the opportunity to jump back into the cab and drive off.

Lucky for Trigga, his club wasn't but a few blocks away. He took off hobbling. On the way there, he tried to call Keisha, but she wouldn't accept his calls.

THE MOMENT TRIGGA walked into his club, he knew something was terribly wrong as he looked around for Red. What he saw blew his mind. First, there was the loud smell of weed permeating throughout the club, and on the pole was one of the fattest, bad body chicks he had ever seen. At first, he didn't recognize her, then upon close examination, it dawned on him who it was. A stripper name Kreme. She had just had a baby about two weeks ago, and it looked like it.

"Wha-da-muthufuck!" Trigga exclaimed and rushed the stage just as one of his waitresses walked by. He snatched her arm so hard, her neck snapped back, causing ringlets of her wig's hair to spray over her face.

"Sheryl, where is Yadi?"

She did a double take at Trigga with his face bruised, arm in a sling. She adjusted her wig and shouted above the music. "She over there," she gestured, pointing as she did a balancing act with drinks on a tray.

"Shouldn't you be in the hospital?" a voice inquired from Trigga's side. Ignoring it, he pressed on but stopped suddenly when he felt a hand on his arm. He grimaced slightly before following the hand up to the woman at his side. It was Lania.

"Naw. Shouldn't you be in school?" he countered with a raised brow. Lania sighed and shook her head.

"No...well, I should but I figured you would be out here sometime soon and that you'd need some help getting this place together."

Both Trigga and Lania looked over to where Kreme was bending over shaking her ass in a patron's face as he smacked it hard on the side. Trigga's lips curled up in disgust as he watched her stomach shake more than anything else on her body.

"Bitch looks like she fresh out the damn hospital from delivering her damn baby but she done popped her big ass on the stage. What da fuck is Yadi doin'?!" Trigga grumbled as he walked by Lania and over to where Yadi was sitting, grinding up on a man who appeared to be seconds away from an orgasm. Around her was a crowd of men, staring at her with lustful eyes as they licked their lips and waited for their turn.

Oh, I see what the hell is going on, Trigga thought to himself. *She fuckin' up my club by puttin' these lame ass chicks on stage so her ass can make all the damn money.*

"YADI!" Trigga yelled so loud that her movements stopped instantly. Yadi's eyes flew over to where Trigga stood glaring at her and then widened with surprise as she began to gather herself off of her client's lap.

"Where you goin', baby?" the man called and tried to grab her by her waist but she brushed him off roughly. The surrounding men groaned in unison at their place in line being interrupted due to Trigga.

"What da hell are you doin' to my club?" Trigga asked, using his one hand to point towards Kreme as she began another set. "The fuck is she doing up there? I can still see her fuckin' stitches, Yadi! I put you in charge and you got niggas smokin' and shit in here..."

He paused when he saw a Tory, a dancer, walking to the back with one of the higher paying patrons. But what caught his eye was that he was rolling a packaged condom between his fingers.

"...you got chicks fuckin' niggas up in here. What da fuck?"

It wasn't until Yadi's eyes moved behind Trigga that he realized Lania was standing by his side watching and waiting for Yadi to answer as well. He was about to tell her to keep it moving when she jumped in.

"And, on top of that, you removed me from the schedule and haven't let me dance since Trigga's been gone! I have kids to feed and I don't appreciate that shit!" Lania added with fire in her eyes.

"She got a point," Trigga added with a shrug. "And now I understand this shit...so basically you removed all your damn competition so you could destroy my club and make all the money, huh? Take your ass home, Yadi."

"But, Trigga—" she started but Trigga wasn't trying to hear it.

Yadi had been cool with him for as long as he could remember. They met as kids and he always watched out for her, letting her do her thing but making sure niggas never abused the privilege of having access to her body.

But the one time he needed her to look out for him, she let her selfish attitude get in the way. He was done.

"Naw, save it. I'll let you know when you can come back but you no longer in charge of the club. Evidently, I can't trust you to do shit right around here. Pack up and leave," he told her with an even tone.

Lania folded her lips in front of her chest and cut her eyes at Yadi, silently amening everything that was being done. Trigga didn't even move to tell her to leave. In his mind, she had a valid point. Yadi had messed with her money, taken food from her kids' mouths and his as well. Lania was one of the top earners, if not *the* top earner. To have her out for the past few nights meant that there was some money lost from out of his pockets too.

With her hand on her hips, Yadi rolled her eyes at Lania and directed her attention to Trigga one last time before leaving.

"I kept *her* off the schedule because I don't trust that bitch!" she said through her teeth, cutting her eyes back at Lania. "And, if you do, you're making a big mistake. She's foul, Trigga. Believe me."

And with that, Yadi turned around, flipping her long hair over her shoulder as she sashayed back to the locker room. Every man in the club watched with pain-filled expressions on their faces as she sauntered away.

"I don't know what she's talking about, Trigga, but—"

"Lania, can you work? Like now?" Trigga asked as he watched some of the patrons begin to leave. The main event was gone and they were ready to go, too. He needed someone to keep their attention until he could get everything back in order.

"Of course," she answered, placing a hand on his shoulder and squeezing. "Anything you need, I can help with. I used to help run the club that I danced at in Texas. So until you're up to it and you find a replacement for B.J., I got you."

Trigga hesitated for a minute but then thought of what he was dealing with. The club was going to need some serious work and not only was B.J. gone but Keisha wasn't pulling back on her threats either. He had no one in his corner at the moment. His hands were tied.

"I'll take you up on your offer. We can talk later about what I might need you to help with."

As soon as the words left his lips, Lania's entire face lit up like a kid on Christmas. Trigga wasn't sure if the move he was making was a good one or a stupid one. Being from the streets, he usually relied on his instincts but everything he was dealing with concerning Keisha had his mind fucked up. And for once in his life, he had no idea what to do to fix it.

"ive your son a kiss goodnight and then get the hell out," Keisha said as soon as she opened the door, not even waiting for Trigga to use his key.

"Keesh, why the fuck you actin' like this?" he asked as she turned around and started walking down the hall away from him. "What kind of woman penalizes a nigga for tryin' to take care of his fuckin' family? This is bullshit and you know that shit!"

When Trigga saw Keisha stop short, her body going stiff as a board, he knew he'd said too much.

"Oh that's what the hell you think this is, Maurice?" she asked and Trigga winced when she used his government name. Shit was about to get real. It was crazy how he was a gangsta in the streets but when it came to Keisha, he never felt fully prepared for battle.

"No, this is about you putting us *into* danger. With B.J. gone, I've been going through his things and educating myself on what you've been having him do for you at the club. I was only looking so I could help but imagine my surprise when I saw that my husband been investing in some shady shit that puts you right back in the middle of the street shit that almost killed us years ago! You promised me you were done with that shit!"

Keisha's teary-eyed stare hurt him to his heart because he knew she was right. He had promised he would stay out of the game after Cameron was born. But even when he made the promise, he knew that if it ever came down to it, he would go back. When it came to providing for his family, he had no choice. He was her husband but, above all, he was a man. There was no way that being the type of man he was, he would be comfortable with not being able to provide the lifestyle his family deserved. Keisha would just have to get over it.

"I promised you that I would take care of you and that I would protect you, Keesh. And that's what I'm doing," Trigga replied with a straight face and dark eyes.

The decision was made and there was no turning back. Even if he wanted to change his mind, he couldn't. He had only two days to collect the money needed to protect his family. If Keisha didn't agree, then he would have to figure out how to live his life without her until she came around.

"I'm a man and I do what I feel is best for my family regardless to what you think about it. You gone either ride with me or not. That's your decision."

With a single tear falling down her cheek, Keisha brushed it away and shook her head.

"No, that's *your* decision," she replied back quietly. "Say goodnight to Cam and then you have to leave."

Without saying a word, Trigga stood firmly in place and watched as Keisha tried to hold it together while tears ran down her face. She was devastated and it hurt him to the core to know that he was the reason for her pain. But at the same time, he knew he'd rather see her alive than dead. She could be angry all she wanted...at least he knew he was doing what he had to in order to keep her and Cameron safe.

Walking by her, Trigga resisted the urge to reach out and grab her into his arms as he continued down the hallway. As soon as he turned the corner, he heard Keisha's sobs grow into a heart-wrenching wail that tore his soul. Closing his eyes firmly, he tried to ignore the sound of the only woman he'd ever loved crying for relief from her turmoil as he walked into his son's room.

"Cam?" Trigga called out, looking over to where his son lay. He was sound asleep.

Sighing, Trigga walked over to the edge of the bed and bent down to his knees. There was a sharp jolt of pain that ripped through his side as he lowered himself to the floor but it was nothing like the aching in his heart. No man should ever be made to part with his family. Trigga was strong enough to endure a lot of things but this wasn't one.

"Take care of your mama, Cam," Trigga whispered as he watched his son's even breathing. He looked so peaceful and that's how his father wanted him to stay.

"Take care of her until I get back. I love you," he finished but continued to kneel there watching the rise and fall of Cameron's chest. He could have stayed there all night, being comforted by his son's presence but he was running out of time.

Leaning over, Trigga pinched Cameron's nose before standing up and taking a deep breath. He walked out of the room and down the hall to where Keisha stood, wiping tears from her eyes.

"I love you, Keesh. You may not understand it now but everything I'm doing is for my family." Reaching out, he pulled her face up by her chin. "I'm still the same nigga you fell in love with. The one who won't stop at anything to protect you. That's still me."

Sniffling, Keisha bit her lip and looked away. She opened her mouth like she was going to say something and then shut it. She was struggling with her decision and it was then that Trigga realized she wanted him to stay. If he pressed a little more, she would allow him to. But he knew leaving was the right decision. There was more he could do on his own than he could do with her.

"I'll call you," he replied as he pulled away. "Make sure you lock up and keep the alarm on."

Trigga ducked out of the house and closed the door on the devastated look on Keisha's face. She didn't understand now but she would later.

"Queen," Trigga said into the phone as he pulled out of the driveway of his home, glancing at it through his rearview mirror. "Can you have Rodney and a few of his men stationed outside of my crib. Keisha and Cam are there alone."

"I can," Queen replied but there was something about her tone that let Trigga know she was waiting for him to say more. He knew exactly what it was.

"And I'll take the job. Send me all the info and I'll get it done."

12

*I*t had been five years that Trigga had been out of the game but he didn't miss a beat when it was time to perform. The thing about the streets is that it is in you. There was no parting with it at any point. Once a street nigga, always a street nigga. It was in Trigga's blood and it always would be. With that attitude came the audacious mentality of his gangsta's mindset: kill or be killed. He had no intentions of being killed.

As he eased through the streets of Brooklyn, his eyes surveying the road, he watched as business was conducted in a multitude of ways. Corner boys trappin' on the block, completed transactions with ease, whores, scantily dressed, provocative, with hardly any clothes on attracted clients right under his watchful stare and boosters sold stolen goods from out of the trunk of their cars in broad daylight with their hood mantra being "it's not illegal unless you get caught."

Introspectively, Trigga missed the enchanting allure of the streets, the hustlers, the hoes, the danger that was all part of the mystic of the hood, where he had unceremoniously been crowned King of the streets by his peers. Even though he'd been sequestered the last five years at home, his new domain, playing the rule of dad and husband, he knew in his heart as he continued to pass old friends and associate as he drive, he missed his first home. His first love, the place that had indoctrinated him into gangsterism, was Brooklyn. It would always be his first love, like that evil, crazy bitch with the good pussy—that niggas couldn't resist—and, yes, she had even burned him and on a few occasions he had been shot but she would always be his home.

Bringing his car to a complete stop, Trigga killed the engine and checked for his strap, making sure his .9 mm was fully loaded. Then he surveyed the streets scrutinizing every house, every corner, every moving car and person in the vicinity. Longevity in the ghetto, as it relates to living a long life, meant never getting caught slippin'.

Trigga jumped his whip, walking swiftly to a building on the corner that housed four apartments, all of them occupied by the same owner. There was a young kid standing out front smoking a blunt, he wore his hair in blond, large dookie locks. He was dressed in army fatigue. He gave Trigga a quick once over then turned his head and pulled out his phone and began to text someone. Trigga quickly peeped the move at once. The young kid was the Lookout. Unsuspecting to many, the Lookout was a critical element to maintain a successful drug operation.

There was a light breeze in the air as he walked briskly with the scent of rotten stench in his nostrils.

It's stank as hell in this shit, Trigga thought as he stepped over some littered trash. His foot almost landed on a large rat, nearly the size of a cat.

"Wha-da-fuck!" Trigga scoffed and hopped out the way as the huge rat scurried off in the opposite direction. Instinctively, Trigga had pulled out his banger on impulse. He heard a giddy chuckle and looked up. The kid at the front was laughing at him as the blunt smoldered between his fingers.

Trigga's eyes shoot daggers at the young kid as he placed his banger back in his pants and knocked on the door. He was suddenly conscious of the peephole but he had also spotted the camera up above watching his every move as he ran his hand over the coarse, unshaven hair on his jaw. Someone was at the door. He listened to the loud, heavy belts and locked being turned; the place was locked up like tight. Suddenly the steel metal door opened with a clang and Trigga smiled wide for the first time in days.

"Nigga lemme find out you scared of a little ole mouse," Gunplay giddied.

"Nigga that was a BIG ass fuckin' rat, the size of a dog! I almost shot that bitch!" Trigga said dead ass serious.

They both shared a good hearty laugh like old friends reunited. Trigga changed the conversation on a different tempo, happy to see his old friend.

"Gunplay...nigga, what's happenin'? I see you got this bitch on high security, huh?" Trigga reached out and tapped his fist with Gunplay's.

"Ain't shit. A nigga just tryna stay on point, na'mean? These days niggas gotta look out for the po-po, the jack boys *and* another nigga who might start snitching," he replied, leaning out the door to see if anyone was watching them. He spotted his young lookout and screamed on him.

"Poo-Boy, you better not be out here smokin' weed n' shit again when you supposed to be watching a nigga spot. I'ma fuck your ass up next time I see ya!" Gunplay threatened.

"Man, I ain't smokin'," a juvenile voice returned.

Gunplay slammed the heavy solid steel door shut. The sound ached as he belted and locked what looked like at least fifteen locks.

"Come in and let me know what da fuck goin' on. The streets been talkin' and I been hearin' 'em. Word is you got yourself in a hell of a situation, my nigga."

"I'm good. Don't believe everything you hear cause I'm good, son, na'mean?"

Gunplay stepped out of the way as Trigga nodded his head and walked inside. Looking around, Trigga was impressed. Gunplay had knocked down all the walls separating the four apartments and made everything into two large rooms. There were cameras and mirrors everywhere to detect any furtive movements and there was also that distinct smell of cocaine being cut with various ingredients.

The windows all had been boarded up and the concrete floor was barren, the sound of their footfalls resonated as they walked to another door. That was when Trigga spotted a guy, he was tall and muscular and donned dark shades. There was a deep gash on the side of his forehead, like he had been in an ugly knife fight. He was dressed in all black as he stood stoic, but Trigga could feel his eyes watching him with every step.

They walked in adjoining room, this room was more sophisticated, more elaborate in terms of detail. There were people busily working and the hushed murmur of voices rang in the air. From somewhere on the other side of the room, the perpetual sound of a money machine whirred as a guy dressed in a simple white t-shirt and blue jeans fed the machine money. On the table in back of him, there were large neatly wrapped bundles of money. There, another armed gunman stood, watching...

In the center of the room there were several tables, covered with all types of drug paraphilia and opened kilos of coke, heroin, measuring spoons, mixing bowls. Next to the tables were discarded wrappers in large garbage bags. But what really got Trigga's attention was one of the four females that stood butt-ass-naked as they packaged cocaine adroitly like skilled packagers on an assembly line. "Tamra?! What da fuck?" Trigga exclaimed as he pointed a finger at one of female workers causing the armed guards to walk over towards him. Trigga paid him no attention as he yelled from the other side of the room.

"Tamra, da *fuck* you doin' here?!"

Tamra blushed and turned her head, causing her large pendulous breasts to bounce with her sudden movement.

"You know her?" Gunplay said while simultaneously shoving his henchmen with the gun to go back to work.

"I told you I had another job!" Tamra shouted above the whirr of the noise in a singsong voice as she blushed with embarrassment. Her face was totally flushed red.

"Hell yea, I know her! Dat bitch work at my club," Trigga said, answering Gunplay.

"Fuck outta here! She told me she worked at the hospital during the graveyard shift to help take care of her grandma."

"She lying! Dat bitch a stripper. Look at all them tits and ass," Trigga said then added, "You fired, Tamra! Don't bring your black ass back to work."

"Don't do that," she whined with a sour disposition as she threw both her arms in the air in despair. The other three ladies just stood around looking perplexed with the exchange of words.

As Trigga and Gunplay strolled off, Trigga commented to his friend under his breath, "Yo, B, you need to fire her ass. Bitch told me she was working at the hospital too."

Gunplay roared with laughter than added, "Uh,-uh, naw, I'm staying outta dat. She work her ass off. Plus she fine as fuck. Sounds like you in your feelins nigga."

"Never dat. Just can't stand a chick that take my kindness for weakness. And I can't deal with all that lying shit. The bitch used to leave work, talking 'bout she had to rush home to take care of her ill grandma. She used to hit me up for money all the time too."

Gunplay couldn't help but laugh some more. They passed another table with more nude chicks working feverously at measuring and bagging the coke. It was like an assembly line operation and there stood another gunman like a sentry, alert and hulk-eyed, watching two females at the front door with shrewd alertness.

The two other women were chained by the ankles as they stood on the separate end of the large room. They looked haggard and malnourished. You could see deep purple and red marks on their legs from where the leg irons were leaving ugly bruises. Trigga stopped in his tracked and raised a brow.

"Damn, playboy, what kind of slave shit you runnin' in here? You got hoes tied up and some mo' shit." Trigga asked as he motioned over to the women who were chained around their ankles.

Gunplay followed his gaze and then laughed when his eyes fell on what Trigga was looking at.

"Man, them two bitches right there thought they was slick as fuck and damn near bankrolled a nigga."

"Word?" Trigga asked, his eyebrows raised.

"Them two hoes right there had been stealing from me and that shit almost put me out of business. I had been trying to catch they ass stealing for months but couldn't catch 'em. But then, one day, I figured out how they was stealing my shit! A couple ounces a day... that shit added up to about ten thousand dollars a week and more!"

Trigga couldn't help but shake his head at him before he asked, "How the fuck you catch 'em? Damn, that's a lot of coke! That can put a nigga whole operation outta business."

"Man, them hoes was wrapping the coke up in small bundles and swallowing the coke and going home shitting it out. I was fucked up for a minute, I even shot one of my cousins thinking he was cuffing the product on a nigga and come to find out it was them bitches."

Gunplay said loud enough for them to hear as he pointed to the females, it was then that Trigga noticed the short chubby one had a black eye. The other one was drop-dead gorgeous with a cinnamon complexion. She was tall and slender, a redhead with freckles, beautiful, even though you could see her rib cage like she was starving. She had an overbite that give her sex appeal in a nerd kind of attractive way.

"So I guess you gotta charge it to the game."

"Charge it to the game my ass! Them hoes working here for free until they pay back all my damn money. In a few years they should be finished paying it off."

"Is you serious?" Trigga asked and sped up his pace. Everything about what crazy ass Gunplay was doing had 'Federal Indictment' written all over it.

"Damn right I'm serious! They lucky I didn't slump both they fuck ass for stealing my shit, as it is. I have them on food and eating restrictions."

"Hell naw'll, nigga, them crackas gone bury your ass with time," Trigga laughed as he followed Gunplay through the building.

"Shit they would bam my ass anyway if they come in here and find out we cooking crack, mixing heroin and cutting up dope. I got a meth lab in the basement. Wanna see it?" Gunplay added with glee in his eyes.

"Fuck naw'll," Trigga grumbled. "I'm ready to bounce man. You gone get a nigga a federal charge if them crackas run up in here, and I'm standing in the trap. I'm an innocent bystander."

Gunplay nudged Trigga with his elbow and snickered, "Scary ass nigga! I remember you used to be a goon. Now that 'at home dad' shit got you shook."

"No, just made me smarter. For real, it looks like you the one shook with this whole operation."

"Hell naw'll nigga, them bitches taught me a lot! I have a state of the art security system. They can't take five steps in any direction. I see everything now. They gotta call me to take a piss," Gunplay bragged before waving Trigga over to a sitting area to the side.

There was a couch, a big ass TV and an Xbox One along with a small fridge. Gunplay motioned for Trigga to sit down and then opened the fridge, which was filled with Heinekens and a few bottle waters. He offered Trigga one; he shook his head 'yes' and took a seat. It was obvious his mind was elsewhere.

"A'ight," Gunplay said as he opened one for himself and took a long swig. "Now tell me who we 'bout to run up on. I told you earlier the streets been talking."

Trigga sighed before speaking. "Long story short, I gave a nigga some of my money to invest in some shit that would have flipped it. The club has been losing money and I needed an easy come up. Now that B.J. has been killed—"

"Word?" Gunplay asked with his eyes wide and Trigga nodded his head.

"He was killed in the shoot-out at the club. Now he's been killed and the nigga who I gave my money to ain't answerin' his fuckin' phone. I need to pay him a visit to get my shit back. I had the savings we put aside for Cam wrapped up in that shit. I gotta get it back or Keesh gone have my ass, na'mean?"

One of the women shackled interrupted. "Gunplay, I gotta use the bathroom."

"Bitch, you better go in that bucket like you been doing and stop calling my fuckin' name," Gunplay grunted at one of the women who had stolen from him.

"But ain't no toilet paper," she whined in a voice that made Trigga's skin crawl.

"You should have thought about that before your kleptomaniac ass stole my dope! Use a piece of that garbage bag like you been doing," Gunplay crassly stated with grit.

"Humph! I hate you!" she retorted.

Gunplay shook his head dismissively as he took a swig of his beer and turned focusing his attention back on his friend.

"Now what was you sayin... oh, yea. If it's one thing I know, it's that Keisha don't play when it comes to Cam. You know I got your back but don't do no shit like this again."

Silence loomed for a minute as Gunplay took another long swig of his beer and watched as the women continued counting money at the tables and bagged up his dope. The one older chick with the black eye squatted over a bucket and strained to take a shit. Then, suddenly, he turned to Trigga with his brows bunched up into a frown.

"What kinda shit were you investing in that was worth using Cam's savings? Must have been some good shit. What you don't fuck with me no mo?" Gunplay asked with his piercing eyes trained on Trigga's face as he took a long swig from his beer.

"No, why you say that? You see I'm here!" Trigga responded though he was fully aware where the conversation was going.

"Yeah, you here but you on some other shit, my nigga." Gunplay's words were laced with a heavy dose of accusations.

"Other shit?"

"Yea, now that I think about it, you gone get some work from an off-brand ass nigga instead of fuckin' with me, your boy. And you know a nigga was going to break bread and throw you a little s'umptin extra on the strength I fucks with you hard, yo," Gunplay stated with steel in his voice.

"So what you saying?" Trigga questioned, starting to get heated. "Just cause a nigga didn't come to cop no dope from you shit ain't gravy between us?"

"Naw'll what I'm saying is, you done let some lame ass nigga walk you for your work and now you here expecting me to risk my shit when you don't ever really fuck with me!" Gunplay explained with vim as he raised up and stood. To his surprise, so did Trigga, only he was all up in his chest, face to face, only inches away. Just that fast, as was the norm between them, the moment had become volatile.

Sensing the sudden change in mood, two of Gunplay's henchmen, armed with assault weapons, an AK-47 and R-15 rushed over and aimed at Trigga's head. One of the females screamed!

"Y'all chill! Chill!" Gunplay shouted at his men. The sound echoed like they were in a tunnel.

"So this what kinda time we on, my nigga?" Trigga threatened in a guttural tone that sent a shiver down Gunplay's spine as he felt the barrel of a gun nudged against his ribs. It was reminiscent of their last deadly altercation. Back then, Trigga had beat him to the punch and he'd done it once again. He'd always been quicker on the draw.

"Fuck!" was all Gunplay could say as he made a mental note to start having everybody searched down before they entered his shop. Even Trigga.

"You good, bossman?" one of the henchmen asked. He was one of Gunplay's best but he hadn't even detected Trigga's banger pressed between Gunplay's ribs because the two men were standing too close together.

"Yea, I'm good. Go back to your stations." Gunplay replied while never taking his eye off Trigga who was still pressed up close to him.

With grit in his voice Trigga said, "See nigga? You rappin' slick but I could have gun-smoked your ass again. Just like last time." Trigga chuckled a little, lightening up the mood.

"Not really! I knew you had that banger on you," Gunplay lied as he took a hesitant step back, looking at the Chrome-plated pearl handle .9 mm aimed at his chest. He couldn't help but smile to himself. Trigga had diffidently earned his nickname.

"You know I was just fucking with you, right? Your problem is my problem, homie," Gunplay said and extended his hand for some dap. Trigga banged his fist against his hard enough to make Gunplay wince noticeably.

"Nigga, you was dead-ass serious. You was in your feelings about this fuck ass dope."

"It is what it is, just like you would be. I'm over here basically throwing bricks at the chain gang by selling this dope but instead of foolin' with me, your ass spending the chips with the enemy."

"The enemy?" Trigga creased his brow, befuddled.

"Yeah, he the enemy now. Let's go get his fuck ass and get them chips back, B."

Trigga couldn't help but crack a smile. Gunplay would forever be his nigga even though they constantly fought like brothers ever since they were teenagers.

Suddenly, the female that was taking a shit a top the bucket complained like she was on the brink of hysteria.

"Gunplay, this damn trash bag got my asshole raw!"

Jumping, Gunplay whipped around and sneered at her.

"Bitch, didn't I tell you to stop calling my name!"

13

Nothing about life without Trigga felt the same. It wasn't natural. Every since the first time they'd laid eyes on each other, Keisha knew there was something about him that she wouldn't be able to shake. They were meant to be. And she knew she was dead wrong for kicking him out. Trigga was a product of the streets. It was where he felt most comfortable and it would always be that way.

The past five years, she knew that he was just playing a role. He was happy being with his family but she'd be lying if she said that there weren't days when he seemed bored. He had calmed down for her sake but if she wasn't in the picture, Trigga would still be running the streets, working for Queen. Things got tense for the both of them, especially around the anniversary of their child's birth and then sudden death. He used to relieve his stress in the streets but now he didn't even have that. He had compromised a lot for her sake and he never complained about it...until now. It wasn't fair to him and Keisha knew it.

For this reason, she was heading to the club to speak with Trigga and let him know that she was wrong for kicking him out. They needed to talk things out and she was ready to do that. Or at least she was before she walked in and saw Lania's scantily clad body prancing around the club like she owned the place.

"What are you doing here?" Keisha asked as she walked up on her.

Cocking her head to the side, Lania tossed Keisha a small smirk that instantly made her blood boil.

The main thing that she didn't like about Lania was that she always seemed to be testing her. She didn't know her place and there held absolutely no respect for Keisha anywhere in her body. She considered herself Keisha's equal and that meant that she was waiting for the opportunity to take her place in any area she could. She had the mentality of a side bitch that was pushing hard to be in a main bitch's place.

"I'm here because Trigga wants me here," she replied back in a way that seemed mostly polite had it not been for the sly grin that was still plastered on her face. "He asked me to take on a few extra responsibilities to help him out. He's been kinda stressed lately so I been helpin' him handle that any way I can."

"What?" Keisha asked with a frown.

Her eyes surveyed the club and she had to admit that the club did seem to be running much better than it had when Yadi was in charge. While Trigga was in the hospital, Keisha had stopped by a couple times to check on everything. She could tell Yadi was running it into the ground but she'd had too much to worry about and getting the club right while Trigga was in the hospital wasn't at the top of her list.

"Where is Yadi?" Keisha inquired, bringing her attention back to Lania who was still watching her with a smug look on her face.

"I put her on the schedule for later on tonight. Around 10."

Keisha frowned and looked Lania up and down in disbelief. "*You* put her on the schedule? Who has you doing the schedule? You only been here... what, a couple weeks? What makes you think you're qualified to do anything around here?"

With her dark eyes sparkling with pleasure, Lania chuckled a little and took a glance around the club before dancing her eyes back over to Keisha's face.

"What makes me think I'm qualified is that Trigga said I was. He trusts me to handle things while he's gone and I'm willing to do whatever he needs," Lania replied suggestively as she licked her lips and peered into Keisha's eyes.

Keisha became aware that many of the dancers were still doing their thing but were also casting curious glances in their direction as they wondered what was going on between the boss' wife and his new head bitch in charge. The tension in the air was so thick it could be cut with a butter knife. Keisha could feel her cheeks heat up as a thin sheen of sweat covered her face. Her temper was flaring up faster than she could hold it down and she knew that she was seconds away from snatching Lania by her hair and catapulting her across the room like a ragdoll if she didn't hurry up and calm down.

"Keesh!" a voice called. Before Keisha could react, someone grabbed her by her arm and whipped her around. Keisha's eyes fell on Tory's mocha brown face. Her eyes were wide as she cut them back and forth between Keisha and Lania who was still holding the smirk on her face as she placed her hands on her wide hips. Sucking her teeth, Tory gave Lania a look before pulling Keisha away.

"Don't lose your shit over this bum bitch," she warned her as she thrust her head back at Lania. Keisha clicked her tongue against her teeth and tried to pull away to go after Lania but Tory held her firmly and shook her.

"Don't! She's disrespectful as fuck, I know. But you've got to trust your man. He's not stupid and he knows what he's doing," Tory told Keisha, giving her a stern look. Or a look that was about as stern as she could give being that she was standing in front of Keisha stark naked with neon green paint on her nipples.

Keisha was about to reply back but Tory continued on before she could.

"Plus, look at what's she's done to the club! When is the last time you've seen it this packed during the week? The bitch knows her stuff. Just count that green as it comes in and *relax*. If anything, that bitch is workin' for you! Trigga ain't goin' nowhere."

With her eyes still on Lania as she sauntered through the club with her tight ass swaying back and forth in front of the patrons' hungry eyes, Keisha nodded her head. Something didn't feel right about the entire situation concerning Lania. It just wasn't the feeling in the pit of Keisha's stomach that Lania had her mind set on making Trigga her own. She wasn't the first woman with that goal in mind and all before her had failed. There was something else about her that Keisha didn't like but she knew it would show itself soon.

"Go on home and relax. Call your hubby or something. I'm here with my eyes open and I'll let you know if I see anything out of the ordinary," Tory assured Keisha. She reached out and touched her on the shoulder, pulling Keisha's attention back to her comforting eyes.

Relenting, Keisha nodded her head and licked her dry lips as she forced herself not to look back at Lania Crazy enough, she could feel Lania's eyes boring into the side of her face but Keisha wouldn't give her the satisfaction of knowing that she was indeed bothered about her presence.

"You're right," Keisha finally said to Tory. "I'm not worried about no basic bitch. I'll see you later."

Tory nodded her head and tossed Keisha a small but encouraging smile. Pulling out her cellphone, Keisha took one last look at Lania who was no longer staring at her but walking around the club chatting with the bartender as if she ran things.

That bitch has to go, Keisha thought, pursing her lips as she waited for Trigga to answer the phone.

But he didn't. After dialing his number again, it still eventually went to voicemail after a collection of rings. Either he was ignoring her call or was too busy to answer. Either way, Keisha was not pleased.

What is going on with you, Trigga? she pondered as she got into the car and drove away from the club. Something was terribly wrong in their relationship and for the first time since becoming Trigga's wife, she was unsure whether or not it was something that could be fixed.

14

"Feels just like the old days, huh?" Trigga said as he pulled out his weapon and checked it out before placing it in the small of his back. Gunplay blew out hot air through his nose, which made Trigga chuckle a bit before exiting the car.

"Nigga, you always in yo' fuckin' feelings. What your issue now, Gunplay?" Trigga asked, nudging Gunplay in the side as they walked up the stairs to apartment 475 where they were told the man Trigga was looking for stayed.

"My issue is that you always hit a nigga up on some shit like this. I like blastin' on muthafuckas and shit but why the only time you call is when you need me to bust on some niggas? We can't just hang out or no shit like that? What you too good for a nigga now?" Gunplay fumed and Trigga tried to bite back the laugh that was tickling the back of his throat.

"You like my brother, man," Gunplay continued. "You the only mutha-fucka in this world I know I can really trust with my life and I be feelin' like you be using me or some shit."

"Shut that emotional shit up, Gunplay," Trigga said finally, unable to hold back his laughter any longer. "You know I love you, man. Even though you get on my fuckin' nerves sometimes... and make me feel like I gotta blast yo' ass every now and then. I got shit going on with the club and with Keisha...it's been hard to get out and just chill but you know I got mad love for you, man. With B.J. gone, I might even have a spot at the club for you. Let's just handle this lil' stuff we got here and we'll talk about it."

Gunplay nodded his head, shaking his long blond dreads behind his back before continuing up the stairs. Both of them knew damn well that Gunplay would never work in Trigga's club. They were both alpha niggas, used to runnin' their own shit. It was a wonder they even got along half the time.

Trigga smiled to himself but he couldn't even be mad at Gunplay for being upset about him not being around. That was the difference between he and Gunplay; Gunplay wore his heart on his sleeve. He was more reckless than Trigga and had the worst temper of the two but he was also the one who wouldn't hesitate to let it be known what was on his mind.

"You ready?" Trigga asked once they were in front of the door of the man who was supposed to be taking Trigga's money to purchase enough dope to triple his worth.

Gunplay nodded his head but Trigga hesitated still. He was a little on edge and it wasn't how he normally operated. But with everything that was at stake, he knew he had to move quickly.

Sensing Trigga's apprehension, Gunplay took charge. Backing a few paces away from the door, he aimed his weapon at the knob and prepared to shoot. But then something occurred to him and he lowered his weapon to turn the knob. It clicked and he pushed the door open, giving Trigga a wide-eyed look.

Trigga pressed inside of the apartment, his nose catching the delicious aroma of a home-cooked meal in the air while his ears filled with the pleasant sounds of The Isley Brothers' hit song 'Between the Sheets'. The entire apartment was littered with empty beer bottles and half-smoked blunts. Trigga's heart dropped as he took a quick assessment of his surroundings and cursed B.J.'s memory.

I can't believe this shit, he thought to himself as he looked around at the utter devastation of the room around him. *I can't believe I would give my son's fund and my life's savings to a man living in this shit. But that's what happens when you're desperate.*

Without saying a word, Trigga pushed away his chastising thoughts and tried to avoid Gunplay's gaze as they continued to walk through the apart-ment towards the hall with their weapons drawn, cocked and ready to go.

"Too easy," Gunplay muttered under his breath as they crept to the bedroom where the music was coming from.

A smirk crossed his face as he walked faster, quickening his pace. Trigga sighed and continued after him. Gunplay was used to this life so it still excited him but it had been five years since Trigga had brought down justice by use of his gun. The prickly feeling of anxiety began to creep up the nape of his neck but he shook it off and pressed on. This was the type of shit he was made for.

"Put yo' muthafuckin' hands in the air and wave them shits like you just don't care!" Gunplay yelled as they burst into the master bedroom.

Trigga came in behind him, almost laughing at the sight that his eyes fell on. The man, Floyd, was lying on the bed looking like big ass pile of black-berry jelly fresh out of jar. He was butt ass naked with his large belly jiggling left and right as a frail woman with ghastly eyes and stringy hair bounced on top of his lap, her nearly deflated, pancake breasts waving in the air a few seconds behind the rest of her.

Once her eyes fell on Gunplay and Trigga, a sharp screech escaped her mouth, similar in sound to a cat being skinned with a dull knife, and she jumped straight off of Floyd's lap, leaving a trail of some milky white substance on his thigh. The woman stumbled backwards so fast, she tripped over a shoe and fell backwards, knocking her head on the corner of the dresser. She was out cold. Floyd was a little slower to react, most likely because he was right in the middle of experiencing ultimate pleasure before being interrupted. When his jaundice-yellow eyeballs opened and focused on Trigga and Gunplay's face, he let out a squawk that was an octave higher than the woman who had been servicing him.

"Don't think so," Trigga warned him, placing the barrel of his gun at Floyd's temple when he saw him move towards the drawer on a nightstand at his side. "We ain't amateurs, nigga. Get da fuck up."

"Please—I don't know anything, didn't do shit, won't do shit! Whatever it is and whoever you lookin' for, it ain't me!"

Floyd, who was sweating profusely and shaking hard enough to start a mini-Earthquake, struggled to get up out of the bed, maneuvering with great effort around his rotund belly as Gunplay watched in humored fascination and Trigga in disgust.

"I can't believe this the muthafucka you gave your money to," Gunplay quipped as Trigga kicked at a thong that was on the ground near his foot.

"Everything I heard about him was good and I didn't have time to check things out for myself. Shit been going south at the club," Trigga said with a shrug but he knew there was no getting Gunplay off his case about it.

"You didn't have time to check things out for yourself? Nigga, you changed. This daddy and family shit got you slippin' like a muthafucka," Gunplay replied with a haughty snort.

"B.J. told me he was someone he used to deal with in the past...fuck, I figured I could depend on his word," Trigga reasoned, looking at Gunplay who was still donning a satisfied smirk on his face at, for once, having the upper hand over Trigga.

"Did you say B.J.?" the man asked as soon as he was able to get to his feet. "God rest his soul. B.J. was my friend. We went way back to—"

"Fuck all that 'memory lane' shit you on," Trigga interrupted as he stepped forward and pressed his gun into Floyd's left cheek, pushing so hard that he gave him a temporary dimple. "What I need you to remember is what da fuck is going on with my money. Now if you wanna keep actin' like you ain't the one who got it, I can just kill you and get this shit over with."

Floyd's eyes lit up but Trigga didn't step back. If Floyd didn't cooperate, there would still be hell to pay.

"Oh! I—I know what y—you're talkin' about!" Floyd started as if it was just coming to him. "I—I made a deal with you a few weeks back. You gave me your money...said you wanted to buy some good dope with it. Top quality shit! I—I can get it for you, I just need a little bit more time!"

Keeping his eyes on Floyd, Trigga tried to ignore the heated glare coming from Gunplay's direction and stayed on task. He pushed in closer to Floyd, hovering his tall, lean frame over the man's squatty, chubby body as Floyd shrunk back in fear.

"Nigga, what you mean you need more time? I been callin' you for days. Your phone broke too, huh?" Trigga watched as Floyd's squirrelly eyes shot over to the iPhone on the dresser before returning back to Trigga's face.

"I—I must've not recognized the number. I don' save my contacts in my phone for obvious reasons," he replied with a pressed smile on his face. His mouth opened when he chuckled nervously, revealing two rows of perfectly discolored, brown teeth.

Frowning, Trigga blew out hot air as Gunplay watched the interaction from behind. He'd put his gun away and had his arms crossed in front of his chest as he smirked at the scene before him. This was the first time in all the years that he'd know Trigga that he felt like he was the pro and Trigga was the amateur.

"You been out the game too long," Gunplay taunted. Trigga's body tensed up but he didn't respond. Gunplay was right; he had been out of the game much too long and this situation was evidence of that.

"N—no, you picked the right man for the job!" Floyd tried to convince

Trigga with his eyes wide as he took heavy breaths in through his flappy lips. "Me and B.J. went way back. If you a friend of his, you're a friend of mine!"

"I don't want you doin' shit for me!" Trigga sneered. "Where the fuck is my money at? I need it now."

Floyd's eyes and jaws dropped open. His mouth began to move around but there was no audible sound. Trigga poked him in the gut with the barrel of his gun to encourage him to speak.

"I—I can't get it to you. I already—"

Trigga cocked his gun and Floyd jumped nearly five feet in the air.

"What I mean is...I can't get it to you *today*. I—Tomorrow!" he screeched when Trigga pressed the metal into his cheek. "Tomorrow! I can get it to you then."

Clenching his jaws, Trigga struggled inwardly with what he should do. He couldn't trust Floyd's fat ass any farther than he could throw him but B.J. had, which made Floyd his only chance at getting his money back.

"One day," Trigga said, lowering his weapon but keeping his piercing gray eyes centered on Floyd's face. "Gunplay, can you get someone out here to watch him?"

"Oh, you want my help now?" Gunplay countered. He shot Trigga a narrowed look before nodding his head. "Yeah, as you wish, Trigga. I'll get somebody to make sure this stupid ass muthafucka you trusted don't go nowhere."

There was a groan from the corner as Floyd's chick began to stir awake and Trigga started to back out of the room. There was still a lot to do.

"Tomorrow," he reminded Floyd on the way out. It wasn't until they were in the car that Gunplay finally decided to speak.

"I can't believe this shit, nigga," he started, shaking his head. "You know I run dope all through this city. How the fuck you gone go to somebody else to front you some shit? And to that nasty ass muthafucka of alllll niggas in this damn city. We talked about this shit when we came back from Atlanta. I told you we could team up if—"

"I don't do teams," Trigga interrupted as they drove off. "I do my own thing. No offense to you, but that team shit just ain't how I do it. I do it on my own."

Sighing, Gunplay shook his head and gave Trigga a pointed look. "Well, you see where bein' on your own got you. That fat ass nigga got yo' money tied up and you callin' me to help you get it back."

Clenching his jaw, Trigga continued driving without saying a word. He'd made a good amount of mistakes in the past few days and didn't need Gunplay to remind him of any of them.

"Truth is," Gunplay continued. "You ain't never been on your own. You had Mase and, after him, you've always had me. Stop being so damn stubborn, Trigga. This drug shit ain't you. You a shooter and I need a shooter I can trust with me. And if you gettin' into the dope game, you need me. Just think about it."

Nodding his head, Trigga didn't respond although he knew Gunplay had a point. The problem was never whether or not he thought it was a good idea to team up with Gunplay because it was. The problem was Keisha. There was no way he could return to the streets and fix his marriage at the same time. It wouldn't work.

15

---

*L*ania ran her tiny fingers over his broad shoulders before rolling them down his chest and chiseled abs. She took a deep breath, pulling in his masculine scent. The musky, manly smell was like an aphrodisiac and spoke directly to the flower between her thighs, making it drip with her feminine juices.

"You love me?" he asked in his normal deep and husky voice, complete with the beautiful Texan southern drawl that she loved to hear.

"You know I do, baby," she replied back genuinely as she circled in front of him and sat down on his lap, spreading her thighs to take him in, happily pulling him to her most delicate of places.

Somewhere behind her, in the other room, she could hear one of her younger children yelling her name but she brushed it off in hopes that one of the older ones would handle the child's request. She was too busy finally enjoying being in his presence.

"So what's takin' you so fuckin' long? I entrusted you with this shit because I felt like you could do it. If you can't then you can easily be replaced," he said as he ran his tongue along her shoulder, up until he reached her neck where he sucked gently while making circles against her skin with his tongue.

He delivered his threat so subtly and sweetly that she almost didn't catch the deadly intent in his tone. In spite of being approached with the idea of being replaced, which she knew from experience could only happen in death, she was turned on to the fullest and found herself grinding against him, wanting his body inside.

"You don't need to do that, papi," she whispered as he pulled her up in the air and placed her down, sliding her right onto his erect pole, splitting her ever so sweetly in just the way that she craved. She grinded against him hungrily as she continued to promise her loyalty to him.

"Anything you want from me, I'll do. I swear, you can trust in me," she purred as she began to bounce on top of his lap, each leap bringing her closer and closer to the pleasure she craved.

"You better, Nia. You know I don't fuck around... I know you can do it, just don't start gettin' the game twisted," he continued. "Everything you're doing is for us. You my bitch, right?"

Lania nodded her head as she dripped her sweetness all over him. He grinded into her harder as he tried to guarantee her devotion by giving her the thing she craved the most: his love... or at least the idea of it. There was nothing more that Lania wanted than to be wanted by a powerful man and he was it. But was he still the one she craved the most?

"If he can get that money to us by Friday then we move on to the next plan. If a nigga can pull together a couple milli in a few days then there is more where that came from," he said once their moment was over. Lania yawned as he laid her on the bed and tapped her hard on her plump ass.

"Find out all you can before we make this next move," he ordered as he stood up and walked away.

Lania went to sleep with her thighs still wet from their juices and the sweet, musky smell of their lustful encounter in the air. When she awoke, her sticky thighs and the aching between them was an instant reminder to her that his presence had not been a dream.

"So what you gonna do?" Lania's best friend, Karmen asked, while loudly popping her gum. The sound of her smacking was so loud, it almost felt like she was in the room with Lania rather than on the phone.

"What do you mean? I'm going to do exactly what bae told me, I ain't stupid," Lania replied as she drove down the road towards the club. Her car began making some clicking noise and she made a mental note to get it checked out. From the sound of it, it was on its last leg and she did not want to be flatfooting it around town.

"Yeah but you said Trigga was fine, right? Why not sample what he's workin' with while you're there... I mean, it's part of the job to get him to trust you, right? You might as well... I'm sure your lil' boo thang won't mind," Karmen giggled but Lania shook her head.

"Naw, he'd never forgive me for that shit. He won't have me fuckin' other niggas... even if it does help with the job," Lania replied.

But although her mouth was saying one thing, her mind was saying another. The more time that she spent with Trigga, the harder her job was becoming. And the harder it was becoming to resist him. He had all the traits that she looked for in a man and it was shown in the way he treated Keisha. Even though she was acting like a bitch, he still stood by her. Lania had never met a man like that before.

Although Trigga wouldn't speak about his relationship with her, she'd heard enough conversations between the two to know what was going on and she knew that even a man like Trigga would need someone to speak to when the time came. She planned on becoming that listening ear. And eventually she planned to turn a listening ear to open legs.

"Fuck what he thinks! He's fucked around on you before, hasn't he?" Karmen spewed out the harsh details of her relationship that Lania wanted to forget like it was nothing.

And this is why I can't tell you shit that I'm planning on doin' with Trigga, Lania thought. *Because I don't need you throwing my dirt back in my face.*

"Yes, he has. But we're working on our relationship and I don't want to mess it up."

Karmen sucked the skin off her teeth and Lania could almost see her rolling her eyes on the other line.

"Girl, you better get you some. At least do it for me... because as fine as you say that nigga is, I damn sure need to hear all about it," Karmen said just as Lania pulled into the parking lot of the club.

"I promise if I fuck him, I'll tell you allllll about it," Lania said in a teasing tone with a smirk on her face. On Karmen's line, a female voice picked up in the background. She seemed to be speaking on the phone so loud that she had to be sitting right next to Karmen.

"Damn, this bitch loud!" Karmen snapped but the woman obviously didn't hear a word because she kept right on chatting. Lania could practically hear every word she was saying.

"Yeah she is. I can barely hear your ass but I can hear her," Lania informed her. "It's okay because I gotta go... I'm about to go in to work now."

"Well, have fun. Do all the things I wouldn't do and more," Karmen giggled and Lania laughed as well.

Just as she was about to hang up the phone, she heard the woman on the other line say something that made Lania pause for a minute before hanging up. She was speaking on the phone but she informed the caller that she had just made it to New York.

New York? Lania thought. *What the hell was Karmen doing in New York?*

"Karmen?" Lania called out but the line went dead. Sighing, she made a mental note to just give her a call later.

As soon as Lania got out of the car, she glanced towards the front of the club and smiled wide when she saw Trigga's car parked.

Perfect, she thought. He was just the person she wanted to see.

Lania gripped her duffle bag of costumes for the night under her arm and nearly ran into the club so she could change. Once she was in her sexiest attire, she wanted to speak to Trigga one-on-one.

Yeah, her man was in town and he had been very specific about what he wanted her to do but there was no reason she couldn't have a little fun doing it. What he didn't know wouldn't hurt him.

"Trigga, I—" Lania started but stopped when she heard the sound of Trigga's voice yelling through his office door.

Smirking to herself, she stood in front of the door and listened to him in a way that she'd never before seen him; angry, frustrated and stressed the hell out over Keisha who, obviously, was not letting up on the argument at all.

"Keisha, man, stop this shit! Why the fuck would you even bring some shit like that up? Have I ever gave you a reason to be worried about some other bitch? Have I *ever*? Don't even come at me with that bullshit!"

Lania bit back the giggle in her throat as Trigga paused to listen to whatever Keisha was whining about which, from the sound of it, was her.

I knew all that shit was an act. She was tryin' her hardest to act unbothered by me but I saw straight through that shit, Lania thought to herself as she shook her head.

"I didn't fire Yadi. I sent her ass home because she was fuckin' up my club. Lania had been runnin' it for only a day and already got shit goin' better than B.J. even had it. You just not gone be happy until I'm fuckin' up, huh? You don't wanna help me run this shit but you got so much mouth when it comes to who should. Get the fuck outta here," Trigga continued angrily as he blew out hot air.

Lania smiled to herself as a feeling went through her stomach and spread all the way up to her cheeks, making them hot. Trigga was standing up for her, defending her to his wife. The man who refused to give her any props when she first started was now taking her side in argument against the woman he supposedly loved more than anyone else.

"Is there a reason you're listenin' in to the boss' calls?" an icy, cold voice said to Lania's side.

Turning, her eyes fell right on Tory's snarky, frowned up face. But instead of being embarrassed at being caught in the act of enjoying Trigga going in on Keisha, Lania smiled and then shrugged in response.

"I'm waiting for him to finish up," she replied with ease and newfound confidence. "I just figured once he's done, he'll need someone to talk to. Someone he can trust."

Jutting out her jaw, Tory turned up her nose and walked in closer, using her tall frame as an intimidation tactic against Lania who was a few inches shorter.

"Well, that person ain't you. I know all about you and soon Trigga will, too."

"You don't know shit about—"

Before Lania could finish, Trigga's door swung open and both Lania and Tory's eyes fell on him. His normally bright, gray eyes were hooded and dark, there was a deep frown line etched into the top of his forehead, making him appear years older than he actually was. His jaw was clenched tightly and his temples were throbbing to the point that you could see them at first glance.

"What da fuck goin' on out here?" he asked, deepening his frown. "There a problem?"

"No but—" Lania started but Trigga cut her off quickly.

"Good, because I can't take shit between y'all right now. Everything needs to keep running smoothly," Trigga told them, looking into each of their eyes to make sure they understood. Lania cut her eyes to Tory who she could tell was seething on the inside and waited to see if she would say anything. But, just as she expected, and preferred, Tory kept her mouth closed.

"Nia, I need to speak to you for a minute," Trigga muttered before turning around and ducking back into the room.

A warm feeling fell over Lania and her stomach filled with butterflies at the sound of Trigga calling her 'Nia'. Although she had initially told him that was what she went by, he'd refused to call her that. The fact that he did now made Lania feel that he'd finally started breaking down the wall he'd built between them.

"Anything you need," Lania replied to his back before cutting her eyes once more at Tory who pulled her lips into a thin line. Frustrated, Tory shook her head and then stormed off down the hall, the plastic material on her skintight booty shorts squeaking as she stomped away.

When Lania walked into the office, Trigga was sitting at his desk staring down at nothing in particular with a deep-seated glower on his face. Without saying a word, Lania closed the door behind her and walked behind him, placing her hands on his shoulders as she began to give him a massage.

"What are you doin'?' Trigga griped but didn't move away. Lania noticed that he seemed to relax some as she kneaded further into his shoulders and then down his back, trying her hardest to relieve his stress.

"I'm just tryin' to help. I've been told that I'm good at these," Lania replied with a soft smile as she looked at Trigga through the large wall mirror ahead of them.

Trigga had the mirror installed when he initially moved into the office, telling Keisha that a gangsta always needed to be able to see in front of him as well as behind. As he stared at Lania through it, he felt like he needed to be pushing her away but he couldn't lie and say that he wasn't enjoying the feel of her hands on him, pushing out the knots of tension that Keisha had placed there. Their eyes connected through the mirror and Lania's pulse began to thrum; her blood started to pound in her ears. The room became smaller and Lania's skin began to feel like it was on fire. Trigga hadn't said a word but his eyes were so expressive and so intense that she felt a million emotions.

What the fuck is this man doing to me?

"Feel better?" Lania suddenly asked, a few moments later. It was then that Trigga realized he'd been staring at her through the mirror the entire time.

A war was raging throughout his mind. He knew that he needed to pull away from Lania because it was obvious she was a dangerous woman to have around him, especially with everything going on with Keisha. But when you had everyone you knew blaming you for decisions you made that you thought were for the best, it was nice to have one person there speaking kindness and trying to make things better.

"Yeah I'm good. Thanks," Trigga told her with a straight face before looking away, his focus going to the papers on his desk.

Lania couldn't read his facial expression but she could definitely pick up on the shift in the room. Trigga was feeling her. It might have been in some small way and he might never act on it but it was there and she could sense it. What amazed her, however, was the fact that she knew she was feeling him, too. And her attraction was probably far greater than his.

"I might need you to take on some more responsibilities and work more hours for the next couple days," Trigga started once she sat in the chair across from him. "I have some things I need to deal with and I won't be around to handle the club if anything pops up. You think you can deal with that?"

Lania nodded her head and stared Trigga so deeply into his eyes that it made him feel uneasy. Although he hadn't done anything wrong with Keisha, it felt like he had, being that he was placing his trust in another woman.

But all of this is Keisha's damn fault, Trigga reasoned, shaking away his guilt. *If she was here at my side bein' the rider that she usually was, I wouldn't have to deal with this shit. I wouldn't need Lania to help with shit because Keisha would be here. Here, where she's supposed to be.*

"I got you, Trigga," Lania told him, honestly, the tone in her voice and the feeling in her stomach surprising, even to her.

She couldn't ignore that she was happy to be the one who Trigga could depend on and was hoping that one day she could be more. Reaching over, she placed her hand atop Trigga's but he tensed up instantly. She pulled back before he had a chance to snatch away.

"I'll see you," Trigga said as he stood up and opened a drawer to his right. Lania watched with raised brows as he pulled something out, something that appeared to be a gun, and stuck it behind his back.

"I gotta handle some business but I'll call to check in on you," he said with a grim expression on his face.

"You sure you don't need me to help with anything else?" Lania asked with a pointed look, letting him know that she saw the weapon he'd placed behind his back. Trigga zeroed his eyes in on her face as if contemplating saying something but then changed his mind and shook his head.

"I'll call to check in on you," he repeated before waving her out of the office. Lania backed out the door and watched him as he locked up his office and continued down the hall.

16

Beware of your surroundings, Keesh, Trigga thought as he watched Keisha standing outside of the white Mercedes that he'd bought her for her birthday. Her head was down as she pecked away on her phone, totally oblivious to what was going on around her. As if sensing his words, she glanced up and then sighed as she pushed the phone in her back pocket and surveyed the area around her.

So you do listen to me sometimes, Trigga thought, peering at her with a half-smirk on his face. He couldn't pull his eyes away. He missed his wife.

A picture-perfect image of beauty, Keisha was leaning against the passenger door with her arms folded as she tapped her right foot on the ground while waiting for Cameron to get out of school. She appeared just as tense as Trigga felt. Marriage wasn't supposed to feel this way... not theirs anyway. Trigga had always convinced himself that they'd gone through the rough shit in the beginning so it was smooth sailing from there.

But being without Keisha and his son was far worse than any shootout he'd been involved in, especially because the reason for his distance wasn't because they'd been taken from him but because *she* wanted it that way. He couldn't remember a time since they'd met that Keisha had actually, sincerely wanted him to not be near her; not out of fear but because she made the choice for him to go, thinking it was better for her and their son. It hurt him to his soul.

The bell rang and about five minutes later, Trigga smiled as he saw

Cameron run out of the building with his too-large backpack on his back and his arms wide as the grin on his face before jumping into Keisha's arms. She kissed him on his forehead and placed him in the backseat. After seeing proof that his family was healthy and safe, Trigga pulled out of the parking lot across from the school and tore off down the road. On his lap was his cellphone, which had a text message from the Queen herself pulled up on the screen. The text was an address of where he needed to go to complete his assignment. Against Trigga's better judgment, he'd assured Queen the job would be completed today and even she had voiced her disbelief at that.

"Today?" Queen had repeated once Trigga had told her of his plans. "But that's not how you work... this isn't an easy target. We have help on the inside but it's still not easy. I figured you'd need a week at least."

"No," Trigga replied back emphatically. "It'll be done today. When can I expect payment?"

Queen paused as she thought his question over. Trigga never inquired about payment because he knew she was good for it. But the fact that he was asking and had also decided to complete a job much earlier than he'd ever done before let her know that something was going on with him and it was serious.

"As soon as the job is done," she told him, quickly, but with edge in her tone. "Trigga, if you needed anything you would tell me, correct?"

Clenching his teeth, Trigga squeezed his eyes shut and tried not to get offended by the fact that Queen would even ask him something like that. Everything he got, he earned off his own back. He didn't take handouts from no one and never would. Queen had to know that. Didn't she know what type of nigga she was dealing with?

"Naw," he told her, honestly. "The job will be done. I'll call you when it is."

And with that, he hung up the line.

Trigga pulled into the parking lot of a convenience store and then circled around to the back where he parked his car. The house where the man was who Queen wanted killed was about three blocks up, a short distance for him to run. His plan was simple. Get in without being seen, get a visual of the target, kill him and leave. From the little research he did, he saw that the target never used his alarm during the day because he had too much traffic traveling in and out but that at night, the entire house was locked down like Fort Knox. That told Trigga he needed to move during the daytime hours.

Trigga walked down a desolated street; a light rain had started to fall, misting the city in an ominous gray hue as New York smog rose around him like a dense gloom fog. For the umpteenth time, he took out the crumpled piece of paper in his pocket and stared at the address he had written down when Queen had given him the location of the hit.

"2315 Grove Street," he repeated out loud as he passed an assortment of brownstone homes in the modest neighborhood.

"2310… " he mused.

He was getting close. Then he spotted it, a black Crown Victoria unmarked police car. He stutter-stepped as he looked at the license plate on the back of the car. It was embellished with the American flag and bald eagle decal. Sure as shit it was a Federal agent car.

Trigga could feel his heart pounding in his chest; he didn't have a real plan but it wasn't just that. He was about to attempt to murder a government informant that was being protected by Federal agents.

His pace slowed as he spotted the house, a two-story home, nothing fancy. Except there were burglar bars on all the windows and the front door had a thick screen door, which was obviously placed there to help detour a burglar.

Trigga walked by inconspicuous as possible as his mind churned. There was a method to his madness. He stopped in his tracks and mopped his face with a weary hand to get the rain off his brow but to also gather his thoughts.

A car passed, its occupants looking at him standing in the rain. He continued to walk and accidently stepped in a rain puddle just as a dog began to bark menacingly at him from inside a window of the house next door. Trigga felt nervous and jittery. He took a second to steal another glance at the house, a place he needed to invade for five million reasons, one for each dollar Queen was going to pay him. His mind pondered how could he get inside the fortress of concrete and steel. He couldn't just walk up to the door and knock; he would be greeted by Federal agents.

"Fuck it," he cursed under his breath.

It began to rain harder. Then there was a tempestuous clap of thunder ricocheting across the sky.

Maybe that was a sign for him to go. His thoughts burgeoned with various scenarios. His mind frantically searched for a way complete his job. Again, he came up short. Begrudgingly, he know it was time to give up the mission.

He abruptly turned around, intentionally kicked at the puddle of water; the incessant dog barked, getting the better of him. He threw up the middle finger at the dog. He never saw its master, an old, eighty year white woman who lived alone. Her entire life was based off looking out her window.

Once again, his mind reasoned with experienced rationale. He *had* to abandon the mission. It was too risky. He was ill prepared. And not just that. His gut feeling, his inner intuitiveness, was telling him something was wrong, *terribly* wrong. He had the uncanny feeling he was being watched; it felt like he was being set up.

Was he walking into a trap?

Then it happened!

A car suddenly came screeching to a halt in front of him spewing water and soot all over his clothes. In the beat of an eye, Trigga had pulled out his banger prepared to start blasting. He ducked down to get a good look inside the vehicle, to take aim, as the rain pelted his face.

The vehicle windows were foggy but he could vaguely hear the thump of pulsating music, a Drake and Lil Wayne rap song blared with heavy bass. Trigga pinched his eyes shut, then open, an attempt to clear his vision. Suddenly, the driver's door opened, allowing the music to flow out crystal clear. Was it the target?

Trigga was about to take aim and start blasting until he saw the young white boy's head, full of metallic blond hair, bounce out the car. The kid had something wide and large in his hand. Trigga blinked his eyes, his vision was still getting blurry in the murky rain and smog but he was able to discern the kid had a pizza boxes in his hand. On the rear of the car was a white bright florescent sign that read, Lou's Pizza.

The pizza driver looked up at the house and checked the address on his cell phone. It was then that Trigga realized what was happening. The occupants of the house ordered a pizza.

Then it occurred to him what to do.

Trigga stashed his banger back in his pants and dusted off his clothing. Just as the pizza delivery boy rounded the car, Trigga accosted him with a big ass Kool-Aid smile.

"What took you so long?" he asked, trying to be casual but the delivery guy looked startled as if it wasn't every day he met a black dude in the pouring rain, that anxious to get his pizza.

"I—I—I came as fast as I could, sir."

"Sho'll did," Trigga beamed and stole a glance over his shoulder to check to see if anyone in the house was watching.

"Your bill comes to $29.90."

Trigga reached into his pocket and peeled off $30.

He gave it to the kid as he took the items from his hand. The kid looked from the money to Trigga who raised his hand up to stop him right when he was about to speak.

"Yo, keep the change."

Trigga abruptly turned and walked off in the pouring rain.

∾

THERE WAS A WROUGHT IRON, steel, screen gate that separated the door to where Trigga needed to enter.

This poses a major obstacle, Trigga thought as he shook the rain droplets from his face and mustered the courage to ring the doorbell. Furtively, he eased his banger out his pants and balanced it under the pizza box, exhaling a deep breath as he rang the bell.

It was on!

∾

TRIGGA WAITED as the dog next door continued the bark. Unknown to him, the old lady was staring intently at him from her clandestine post in the window. Suddenly, the door opened with a whoosh of air, causing the metal screen door to rattle. A loud television blared from inside. A short cherub, rotund man with a potbelly stood. He had a scruffy beard. He wore a wife beater t-shirt along with gray slacks. Under his arm was a holster carrying a gun. He scratched his nuts and yawned when he asked.

"How much I owe you?" He scratched some more.

Trigga feigned a smile. "Thirty bucks."

The agent reached into his pocket and took out his money. The entire time, Trigga's heart raced in his throat, he suddenly had the urge to vomit, his nerves were on edge. He had pulled off a lot of capers in his life but nothing compared to this, he was prepared to murder a Federal agent if it came to it.

Suddenly, the screen door opened with a complaint made from rusty steel and old screws. The cop had his hand out the door passing Trigga some crumpled dollars.

Then it happened!

With the agile quickness of an athlete, Trigga sprung into action. Ashe reached for the money, he grabbed the cop's wrist and pulled him forward, striking him upside the head with the butt of his gun. He hit him with so much force and velocity that he instantly opened up a large gash on the cop's skull, spewing blood like a grapefruit hit with a sledgehammer. The cop keeled over backwards and landed on the hard linoleum floor with a thump!

"Oh-mi-gud." The old woman watching from her window next door exclaimed and reached into her threadbare housecoat for her phone to dial 911.

"Frank! Frank! Is that you making all that noise?" a voice called out from down the hall. Trigga's heart did a somersault. Someone else was in the house, another cop. He knew he needed to move fast, time was the enemy that threatened his demise.

"Frank?" The voice called out again.

Trigga moved stealthily. The terror of him being confronted by a Federal agent with a gun and getting shot was heavy on his mind. From the moment his foot went pass the threshold after assaulting an FBI agent, Trigga's crime was punishable by death according to cops' laws.

He tiptoed, moving at a fast pace just as the cop was getting up from the couch. He was a slender man, in his early 30's with a balding head of hair. He wore thick, bifocals that made him look goofy with slender, wiry arms and a gooseneck. He too was strapped with a gun at his side holster. Trigga's first instinct was to kill him but his better judgment told him there was no need unless the cop went for his strap.

"FREEZE! Move and I'ma splatter your ass against the wall," Trigga shouted as he moved towards the cop and relieved him of his gun. The agent didn't resist.

"Where is Willie Hosea?" Trigga asked as his eyes searched the room, hoping there weren't any more cops.

"You know I'm a Federal agent. You might want to think this over."

"Okay, I am. And I'm thinking I don't want you to be a dead Federal agent. Now where is Willie?" Trigga placed his gun under the cop's chin and cocked the trigger.

"I made an oath to uphold the law to do contrary would be insubordination."

"Fuck ass nigga!"

WHAM!

Trigga violently struck the agent upside the head causing his thick bifocals to go careening across the floor. The cop was out cold and landed on his back between the couch and the end table.

Trigga sprung into action!

On the balls of his feet, he moved down the hall, his wet sneakers made a wet whooshing sound with each step from his prior trek in the pouring rain. Past the living room towards a small bedroom, he heard the lasciviousness clamor of lovemaking. He stopped and placed his ear to the door and quickly changed his mind. That wasn't lovemaking, someone was getting fucked... good.

"Yes, bitch!! Yes, bitch take all this fuckin' big dick." The voice was laced with a heavy Spanish accent. Trigga could hear music in the background. As he reached for the door, he hoped it was his victim inside and prayed it wasn't another cop. The house was had several other rooms, the chances of him getting caught or killed were imminent if he didn't find his victim soon.

He turned the door handle open. It snapped open with a squeak, causing Trigga to pulse, standing still, listening...

He opened the door wider, the lustful sounds of wanton sex got even louder. He first step was on some type of mauve carpeting. There was the melodious scent of stale cigarette smoke and musk in the room. He strained his eyes in the lurid light coming from a single bulb on the nightstand.

"Yeaaaahhh, bitch! Take this dick, you fucking cunt. I'ma fuck you in the ass next, long and hard with no grease, no lubricant! Just raw big dick!" the disgruntled voice lamented as Trigga eased forward, trying to make out where the sound was coming from in the dank room. Then he spotted it. The silhouette of a hump in the bed... two people fucking like animals.

Trigga neared, his pulse was racing, heart palpitating. The intuitive clock in his mind was telling him he had been in the house too long. Abandon the mission. LEAVE!

As he got closer, his gun leveled and prepared to start blasting, he could clearly make out the figure on the bed under the blanket cursing and moaning. The man was on top, his bulbous back was large and hairy.

It was it was the once infamous kingpin, Willie Hosea.

CLICK! CLICK!

The sinister sound resonated like snake eyes thrown at a dice game as Trigga cocked the gun, dropping one in the chamber.

The figure stopped stroking in mid-hump and raised his head, looking up. At that very moment, Trigga thought he heard a staccato of car door been slammed outside the window along with the muffled sound of voices. Again his inner voice was telling him to leave but he didn't. Instantly, he reached down and pulled the blanket off his victim. But not even he was prepared for what he saw next.

"Wha-da-fuck?!"

17

Willie Hosea reared his head up. He was all sweaty, his chubby cheeks were flushed angry red with deep creases in his brow. He was a mammoth of a man, nearly four hundred pounds, it seemed. He snorted heavily, breathing like a Hippopotamus, and resembled one too, with his large head and tiny small eyes ensconced inside a face only a mother could love.

What Trigga found so fuckin' offensive was Willie was on top of an imitation, Kim Kardashian blow up doll with big tits and had been fucking it hard and vigorously, like it was a real woman.

"Pervert ass, nasty muthafucka!" Trigga spat with venom.

"Fuck you doing in here?!" The big man raised up, his voice thick like thunder as he got up off the doll. The massive blubber on his body shook like jelly. The hair on his chest and back looked like he was wearing a rug.

Disgusting ass rat, Trigga thought as he scrutinized the kingpin turned snitch.

Then Trigga lowered his tone, sinister like Lucifer whispering in the dark, "I come to send you to your maker. One-way ticket, you fuck ass rat. I'm still tryna figure out how a kingpin can turn snitch."

Willie's eyes got big as saucers as he flailed his meaty arms to ward off a bullet.

"Nooo! nooo! I got money! Plenty money! How much they pay you? I can double it, triple it. Whatever you want. I can pay it. I'm a billionaire. I'm rich!"

"You're a rat, Willie. You cooperated with authorities and you're gonna die, right here, in this shitty, cum-stained room with your blow-up doll. Say a prayer."

"If you take me out of here, I'll give you twenty million dollars! I swear, on my life—"

"Your life is over, Willie."

Trigga aimed the gun, close range, and shot him in the head.

BLOCKA!

The sound of the gun reverberated so loud in the small confines of the room that Trigga's ears rang. He couldn't be sure but he thought he heard noises coming from somewhere in the house. He rushed over and peered out the door and sure as shit, police had knocked down the front door and what looked like a platoon of cops was entering. He quickly rushed over to the window and jumped out the glass, cutting him in the process.

As soon as he landed on the cold, wet grass, a fusillade of shots were fired at him with bullets whistling pass his head. By then, the rain was coming down by the buckets, making visibility nearly impossible. Trigga got up bleeding badly from the cut in his side and took off running.

"SHIT!" Trigga cursed as he ran down the street as quickly as his legs would carry him.

He was sweating profusely and the wound in his side was delivering a constant shock of pain through his body. His shirt was soaked with blood and, although he was applying as much pressure as possible, the more he ran, the more blood flowed. Never in life had Trigga butchered a job to the point that he'd done that one. He'd been careless. But never in life had he been so desperate to complete an assignment that he'd rushed in without a proper plan.

Trigga hobbled the distance back to the convenience store where his car was parked; feeling like he'd traveled twenty blocks instead of only three. In front of the convenience store stood three old Black men, each holding an open can of beer and wearing ripped and dingy clothing as they stared with interest at Trigga.

"Aye, man, you need some help?" one of them asked. He was missing so many teeth that he whistled as he spoke. Trigga eyed him as he scratched at the crotch of his dirty and worn overalls and peered at him along with his two friends.

"Naw, I'm good," Trigga replied back, turning away as he continued to jog to the back of the store. But when he got there, he was surprised to see that his car was gone!

"FUCK!" Trigga yelled as he looked around in disbelief. But the evidence was clear...it had been stolen. The skid marks where still on the ground, painting the cruel story of what had occurred. His car was gone.

"Shit!" Trigga cursed again and kicked at some gravel on the ground beneath where he stood.

Then his heart dropped when he heard sirens in the distance. He looked down at his clothes with a haunted look on his face before glancing back over at the drunken old men standing at the entrance of the convenience store. He had to get away before he got locked up for the crime he'd committed. Anyone with eyes would know he was involved once questioned.

"You sure you don't need no help now, young man?" one of the other men asked as the other two began to chuckle.

Turning around, Trigga didn't reply before taking off down the street, ducking behind some bushes as he ran as quickly as he could away from the convenience store, eager to put some distance between himself and his crimes. Winded, pain-stricken and nearly at his end, Trigga was just about to find a place to hide so he could lay down for a while and catch his breath when he heard a car approaching where he stood. When he picked up on the sound of the engine slowing, his eyes darted around attempting to find a place he could hide but then he heard a voice that put him at ease.

"Hey... why don't you get in?"

Stopping in his tracks, Trigga turned towards the voice and locked eyes with Lania.

"Da fuck are you doin' here?" he asked, suspicion curling his brow, but then the sirens got louder.

The police were heading in his direction, making his choices very limited. Before Lania could answer, he jumped in the car and closed the door just as two patrol cars turned around the corner and shot off down the street, driving right by them. As Trigga stared at the cars, he was certain that the men at the convenience store had told them that he was on foot.

"I followed you earlier... I knew that you were up to something and I had a bad feeling about it. Good thing I came, huh? You're bleeding," Lania whispered as she looked down at Trigga's soiled shirt and his bloody hand that was covering the deep gash in his side. "I gotta get you some help."

"I'm not goin' to no fuckin' hospital," Trigga told her but she simply nodded her head.

"I know... and I'm not taking you to one."

"You takin' this shit kinda easy," Lania said with a light-hearted chuckle as she cleaned out Trigga's wound. "I've seen even the hardest niggas start cryin' like a little bitch from cuts much less than this."

She began to laugh but Trigga kept his face straight as he watched her tend to his injury. To say he was uncomfortable was an understatement. He was shirtless and sitting in the bedroom of Lania's apartment, on her bed, while she cleaned and packed the area where he'd been cut.

But what bothered him was the fact that he couldn't stop his eyes from roaming over parts of Lania's body that he shouldn't have been staring at: the top of her supple breasts, her juicy, tempting lips, her perfectly flat belly that was partially exposed from out of the bottom of her half-shirt. The soft, tender touch of her soft fingers against his skin felt good in contrast to the stinging pain that he felt everywhere else on his body. Once again, he found himself cursing the weak side of him, the side that felt comforted by the touch of a woman who seemed concerned for his well-being. But still, she wasn't Keisha.

"You this serious all the time?" Lania asked him with her head cocked to the side. She had finished covering his wound but Trigga was so deep in his thoughts he hadn't even noticed.

"What do you mean?" he asked and then immediately regretted posing the question. He didn't have time for small talk.

Smiling, Lania leaned in close and Trigga couldn't help noticing the hint of cinnamon on her skin and the vanilla in her hair. He blinked hard, telling himself to come back to his senses. Everything about this moment was sending off warning alarms in his mind.

"I mean, that serious expression you always have on your face. Like you're afraid to smile... I'm not a bad person. You don't have to be afraid of me, okay?"

Licking her lips, Lania stared deeply into Trigga's eyes, feeling positive that her charm was working on him. He was tense and she could tell he was fighting himself within his mind but the fact that he was battling let her know that she had a chance. His love for Keisha was strong but Lania knew that stress was a beast. Trigga was in a situation where he felt like he was backed against a wall and had no one in his corner. No one but her.

Even the strongest of creatures didn't want to be alone. And Trigga didn't either. After vowing his life to Keisha, Trigga didn't think that he'd ever be in a position where he didn't have her soft, feminine body and strong will by his side to comfort him while he was making the toughest of decisions. But here he was... and Keisha was nowhere to be found.

"Thanks for this," Trigga said, pointing down to his bandage as he moved to grab his shirt. "I gotta get goin' so I'll see you at the club."

"You can't wear that," Lania told him, snatching at the shirt before he could get it. Let me wash it or something first. It's covered with blood."

Looking at Trigga, she noted the look of discomfort on his face and then sighed. "Or, you know what...I probably have a big shirt somewhere in here from the gym or something that I can give you so you can get going. Since you're in such a hurry. I'll just—"

Before Lania could finish her sentence, the shrill sound of a baby's cries pierced through the air followed by a knock on the door. Trigga lifted one brow and glanced at Lania who began to walk out of the bedroom door.

"It's my neighbor. I'll be right back," she informed him as she left, leaving Trigga in the middle of her bedroom.

A few seconds later, Lania returned and, in her arms, was a small baby, probably only about six months old. A beautiful baby girl. Trigga's eyes locked on the child who looked just like her mother, except for her beautiful bluish-green eyes that gave her a peculiar look next to her olive, sun-kissed skin. Trigga couldn't help but look at her and think about his own daughter, the baby girl that he and Keisha had lost. The raw emotion showed through Trigga's eyes and Lania noted that there was an attachment he had to her child, although she wasn't sure why. There was a backstory there.

"Can you hold her for a minute? I have to find some cash and pay my neighbor real quick," Lania asked him, nudging the grinning child into his arms. Trigga grabbed her into his arms, ignoring the throbbing pain in his side.

The child giggled and reached for him as he gazed into her face, unmoving and unblinking. Time had shifted and took him back to the few moments he spent holding his baby girl before she passed away. Those were some of the most precious moments of his life. Moments he'd never get back. Sage would have been three now, much older than the child he was holding but, as he held Lania's child in his arms, the memories of the short time he spent being her father were as strong as ever. His eyes misted with tears but he sniffed them away as Lania walked back into the room.

"Here," Trigga said, pushing the baby into her arms.

Without saying another word, he bolted down the hall and out of the door, pulling his phone out of his pocket in the process. He needed to call Keisha, not just to see what she was up to but also to be comforted by the warmth of her voice. Being reminded of the child they'd lost was messing with his mind. He needed her to calm it.

"Hello?"

"Keisha..." Trigga started and then ran his hand over his face and sighed. "What are you—"

"Trigga, I have to call you back, I'm on the other line and it's important," she told him, instantly pissing him off to the fullest.

"Who can be more important than me, Keesh? You don't have two seconds to give to me?" he asked as he tried desperately to keep his tone low.

"Trigga, don't do this right now. It's important and I need to g—"

"Trigga, you ready to go? I grabbed your shirt off the bed..." Lania's voice trailed off when Trigga turned and stared at her with wide-eyes, signaling for her not to talk.

"Who was that?!" Keisha yelled in his ear. "She got your shirt off her bed... is that Lania? What the fuck you doin' at her house, Trigga?"

Closing his eyes and gritting his teeth, Trigga tried to calm his nerves. This wasn't what he wanted to deal with at the moment. He had called Keisha to put him at peace but she was stressing him out more than ever. He would have been better off not even bothering to call.

"Didn't you say you needed to tend to some shit? That you got somebody more important on the other line? Well, handle that shit then," Trigga replied back bluntly before hanging up the line. He shoved the phone in his pocket and then brought his attention back to Lania who was standing behind him with wide-eyes and a stricken expression on her face.

"I'm sorry," she squeaked out as he grabbed the shirt from her hand.

"Not your fault," was all he said. "Can you take me back to the club? You can bring the kid if you need to... one of the girls will babysit between sets. I got my other car over there. When I get it, I'll be done asking you for favors."

Shaking her head, Lania came close and pulled Trigga into a hug she felt he so desperately needed although he still slightly resisted and eventually pulled away.

"Sorry... I just wanted to comfort you because you seem distressed. I just want you to know that anything you need... I'm right here," she vowed looking straight into his eyes.

With a slight nod of the head, Trigga turned around and walked to her car. Smirking from behind his back, Lania swiveled around and walked back into the house to grab the baby and pack up a few things so they could leave.

Keisha is being stupid and, in no time, Trigga will be mine, she thought as she prepared to walk back out the door, trying to wash away the gloating expression on her face.

18

Sighing heavily, Keisha laid across the large, Queen-sized bed in her guest-room and stared with tear-filled eyes up at the ceiling. Ever since Trigga decided that he wanted to choose the streets over his family, she hadn't been able to lie in the bed they once shared. Keeping herself from calling him was becoming harder and harder but after giving in to her need to hear his voice and instead hearing Lania's whiny ass in the background, she was crushed.

She was losing Trigga. She was losing the one man who meant everything to her and the reason why was because of her own fear. Since Trigga had removed himself from the streets, she'd been able to have five years of living a normal life. Five years of not worrying about who was watching them or who wanted to kill them. Five years of not worrying about whether he was going to get caught up in something that would take him away from his family forever. With Cameron in the picture, Keisha's need for a stable, safe life only grew because she had someone else, someone innocent, that she was charged with protecting as much as she could. But now, there was another variable in the mix.

The thought of giving up her life of comfort and stability in order to give her husband back to the streets terrified her. But the thought of losing Trigga terrified her even more. In her heart of hearts, she knew he wasn't cheating. It wasn't like him. But she also couldn't bring herself to be stupid enough to underestimate another woman; especially another woman like Lania.

Picking up her cell phone again, Keisha dialed another number and prayed the person would answer. Being without Trigga reminded her of how few people she had in her corner. Without him, she didn't have many she could reach out to and even fewer she could trust. She'd placed herself in a situation where he was all she had because he was all she thought she'd ever need.

"Heyyy, what's up, Keesh?" Tory answered after the second ring. "You good?"

Biting her lip, Keisha paused for a beat as fresh tears came to her eyes. She wasn't the type of woman to be putting her business in the streets but she was tired of holding everything inside.

"Tory... has anything been goin' on at the club with—I...I think something is going on with Trigga and..." Her voice died off. She couldn't even bring herself to utter the words that had invaded her mind.

The line went silent for a few seconds as Keisha wiped the tears from her eyes and then, suddenly, she heard Tory take a deep breath.

"Keesh, I gotta tell you somethin'," Tory began in a tone that made Keisha's heartbreak. She didn't reply back for fear that she would tell Tory to keep whatever it was to herself. Ignorance was bliss... right?

"Me and Yadi... um, well..." she paused and took another deep breath before pushing the next few words out in a rush. "Me and Yadi are together... we been for a while. Like officially. Anyways, she told me something a while back and made me promise not to say nothing but I'ma tell you anyways."

"What is it?" Keisha asked in a low voice. She flipped over on the bed on her stomach and gave Tory her full attention.

"The day of the shootout at the club, right before it happened, Yadi heard Lania on the phone outside. She heard her saying something about getting some money and then she said something like 'just don't hurt him. I can get you what you need'. She didn't think anything of it until after everything went down."

An icy feeling traveled down Keisha's spine as she processed everything that Tory was saying. She knew Lania was foul from the beginning and here was proof.

"Why didn't she tell Trigga about this?" Keisha inquired further but she already had an idea why.

"Because Trigga chose Lania over her...Yeah, Yadi was fuckin' up while he was in the hospital. But they go way back and instead of him just talkin' shit out with her, he sent her home and put that bitch in charge. She ain't even gave Yadi no hours since she started handling shit but Trigga ain't said shit about it. But yet he was down Yadi's throat for not giving Lania no hours... that's bullshit so Yadi been staying out his business, just like he wants her to," Tory told her matter-of-factly.

"Damn, I'm sorry to hear that," Keisha apologized. "Really, I don't know what's goin' on with Trigga. Shit hasn't been right between us for a while..."

Her words caught in her throat and Keisha's eyes filled with tears again.

"I think it's childish but that's Yadi. But I wanted to let you know so you can watch your back. That bitch is bad news. I don't know what she's here for or what she's up to but she has her eyes set on Trigga for some reason and it looks like he's too focused on whatever other shit is going on to realize that he's fuckin' up."

"Th—thank you for telling me," Keisha said with a grim expression on her face. "I'll give you a call later."

Hanging up the phone, Keisha ran into the room and grabbed the papers that she'd taken from the club after B.J. had been killed and looked through them again. There it was as plain as day but she'd been so focused on the fact that Trigga was getting back into the streets that she didn't even notice it.

The club was losing money... had been for a while. In fact, Trigga had tried every option before eventually deciding to go back to what he did best. She'd been punishing him for risking their safety but the only thing he was guilty of doing was being a man trying to provide for his family in the best way he knew how. And not once had he even mentioned to Keisha that he was struggling to get it done.

19

With one of Trigga's old guns tucked behind her back, Keisha checked the address on her GPS to make sure that she was at the right place. After searching through the paperwork from the club, Keisha found where Lania lived and decided it was time to pay her place a visit. Not to chat either. She wanted to snoop and see what she was up to. After calling the club, she was told that Lania was supposed to be there until closing so that gave Keisha more than enough time to look around before she had to make her next appointment.

Keisha had taught her a while ago how to pick a lock after she kept locking her keys in the house. Even though she had thought it wasn't a necessary skill to learn being that they always kept an extra hidden outside, now she was grateful for it. Keisha was able to break into Lania's apartment with ease after knocking a few times to make sure no one was inside.

The floors were covered with children toys and old bottles. The house reeked of stale milk and dirty pampers. This couldn't possibly be the place that Trigga had been in earlier. Either it wasn't or he'd been so out of it that he hadn't noticed but Keisha was positive there was no way he would be cheating on her with a woman who kept her crib looking like this.

Keisha walked carefully into the bedroom, trying her hardest to look at each place on the floor before she stepped on it. The last thing she wanted to do was to put her foot right into a dirty diaper. Interestingly enough, the master bedroom was spotless... almost as if it hadn't ever been slept in. Dread passed over Keisha as she looked around the pristine clean room. Maybe Trigga *was* cheating on her and had been so focused on getting to the bedroom he hadn't noticed the mess up front.

Stop driving yourself crazy, Keisha, she heard Trigga's voice in her mind. There was no way he cheated on her. It wasn't in him.

After rummaging around Lania's place for over thirty minutes, Keisha finally decided there was nothing to find. Everything seemed normal. There wasn't any evidence that Lania had anything to do with the shootout at the club. Either she was very good at hiding things or she wasn't guilty.

Just as Keisha was putting things back into place so she could make her way out of Lania's home, her eyes fell on a photo on her dresser. It was a small child; most likely one of Lania's, but what caught Keisha off-guard was the haunting bluish-green eyes. Picking up the photo, she peered closer at it, feeling like she was being hit with a spell of déja-vu. The child's face seemed so familiar to her but it also caused a feeling of panic to swell up in her body. She knew that face from long ago. She recognized it from another life, back when she was in Atlanta.

"Stop driving yourself crazy," Keisha said to herself, this time aloud as she placed the photo back on the dresser. But she couldn't help but glance at it once more as she walked out of the room.

"TRIGGA, ARE YOU CHEATING ON ME?" Keisha finally found the courage to ask after thinking about it since she left Lania's house. "Are you cheating on me with Lania?"

"What?" Trigga asked sounding genuinely confused. There was a lot of noise in the background and Keisha couldn't help pressing her ear closer to the phone to try to hear what was going on around him.

"I know you were at her house earlier and—"

"Keesh, more than anything right now, I need you to trust me," he told her using an even tone that Keisha knew only carried the truth in it. He couldn't be lying but, even if he were, she'd believe it anyways. She wanted it to be the truth just that bad.

"Okay," she said as she looked around her. It was crazy that she was asking him a question and wanting him not to lie when she'd been lying to him for quite some time now. But she couldn't yet tell him the truth. She didn't want to hurt him so she had to let things play out naturally. Trigga would find out her truth at the right time.

"Where are you?" he asked, almost as if he sensed how much she didn't want to tell him.

"Um..." she started and paused when she heard his voice coming towards her, the low baritone of the man who had changed her life so much in the past few weeks for the better. Just hearing his voice made her feel jitters in her stomach although she knew that she had to figure out a way to quickly rush Trigga off the phone.

"I have to go," Keisha muttered, talking fast. "I'll call you later. I promise."

With that being said, she hung up the phone quickly before Trigga could object. Staring at the phone in his hand, Trigga called her right back but she didn't answer. So instead of saying it to her face, he waited for the call to go to voicemail and went in.

"Keesh, I don't know what the fuck you up to or who you with but don't think I'm stupid. Bet not be another nigga wit'chu... It's gone be twin caskets for ya'll muthafuckin' ass, fuck with it and see! You better call me back!" he gritted before hanging up the phone.

"Everything okay?" Lania said, rounding the corner into his office. From the look on her face, she'd heard everything.

Without bothering to answer her question, simply because it wasn't any of her business, Trigga was about to remind her of such when his phone chimed. Thinking it was Keisha, he grabbed it and checked the text. But it wasn't.

Time's up, the text read. *In five minutes I'll text you and let you know where to bring the money. Come alone. Don't be stupid.*

Game time, Trigga thought as he clicked out of the message and focused his attention on Lania.

"Aye, I need you to cover the club for the day until I get back, a'ight?" he asked, only halfway looking at her.

"Of course. How's your side?" she inquired, dropping her head to nod at where he'd been stabbed.

"It's good," he said, honestly. "You did a good job fixin' me up."

Smiling warmly, Lania watched Trigga as he pushed a few buttons on his phone. Then he lifted his head and they locked eyes. Her heart beat five times before he was able to pull himself away from her gaze. But even though he was looking back down at his phone, Lania could tell by the tense way he held his shoulders that he felt whatever it was between them. He felt it but he was also doing a good job ignoring it.

"I'll see you when I get back. I need to make a call," he said in a dismissive way. But Lania didn't mind him telling her to make an exit. He'd be telling her to do a whole lot more later.

"Okay," she told him as she stood up and began to walk away. "I'll see you soon."

20

*D*onning a deep scowl, Trigga glanced down at the face of his watch for what felt like the tenth time in the last five minutes. According to the text he'd received, he was supposed to meet the crew that had shot up his club at the location they'd provided for the drop.

Or at least that's what they thought.

Trigga had the money but he'd be damned if he handed it over freely. Gunplay and his goons were hiding in the cut a few blocks away waiting for Trigga's text that the crew had arrived. Once they were there, Trigga would go forth with the drop until Gunplay and his team swarmed in. It seemed like an obvious assault that should have been expected but Trigga had come to the conclusion that the men where amateurs from the way that they had given Trigga an entire two weeks to come up with the cash.

Everybody in the hood knew that the point of a press was to put a nigga under pressure. You didn't give him a couple weeks to freely roam about and figure out how to get his money together. You put the *press* on him, put him under severe pressure to get it done because you had to move quickly. If you gave someone too much time to think things through, that's when you failed.

But here he was, waiting at the drop-off spot and the men were over thirty minutes late. Something wasn't right and Trigga was beginning to think that maybe they were a little smarter than he'd initially thought.

"Fuck!" Trigga cursed as he glanced down the empty street once more before moving out from the alley he was standing in.

Walking out, he looked back and forth, his eyes falling on a few home-less people situated in various spots on the road, paying absolutely no atten-tion to him at all as he ambled about aimlessly. But then his focus fell on something in the corner, right in front of an old building that looked as if it had been a pharmacy over a decade ago.

It was a manila folder that seemed very out of place in the filthy street. With his eyes narrowed in on it, Trigga walked to the envelope, nearly running into a frail older woman with bug-eyes and tattered clothing in the process. She smelled like vomit and old, stale cigars.

As she walked by Trigga, just narrowly missing him, she gave him a very toothy and rotten grin. Without really paying attention, Trigga glanced in her direction and then looked away, ignoring everything around him except the one thing that current had his attention: the envelope. Leaning down, he picked it up and ripped it open quickly.

But when his eyes focused on the photo inside, he almost lost his mind.

Biting back his emotions, Trigga stared at the photo over and over again, hoping to find something in it that would indicate that what he was looking at was false.

It couldn't be true.

Trigga's heart clenched tightly in his chest and he felt the onset of panic in his body right before realizing that he'd stopped breathing. His jaw clamped tightly together as he focused once again on the photo, trying intensely to stop his blood from boiling in his veins. Closing his eyes, he willed the image away but when he opened them back, the photo still remained.

There, in his hands, was a photo of Keisha in the middle of a tight embrace with another man. She was hugging him tightly, her arms wrapped firmly around his neck and her body was pressed close to his. But what devastated Trigga was the time and date stamp on the photo. It was a couple days back around 3 am in the morning and she was standing in front of a hotel. One he'd taken her to often.

What the fuck was she doing with another nigga at three in the morning? Why is she hugging him? And where in the fuck is my son? Trigga thought as he gripped the photo hard in between his fingers.

Squeezing his eyes closed, he crumpled the photo up and placed it in his pocket while cursing Keisha's very existence.

Twin caskets, Trigga thought to himself, repeated the threat he'd issued to her earlier as he walked away. *As soon as I find out who the fuck that is, I'ma put the both of y'all asses in them.*

~

LANIA WAS in the middle of a set when Trigga walked into the club, looking like something was heavy on his mind. The frown that stayed constant on his face was etched deeper than ever before and his eyes were hooded over by his furrowed brows. As he tramped through the club, everyone in his way moved quickly aside to make a path for him. Without saying a word to anyone, he walked down the hall to his office without even bothering to reply to the greeting of some of his most loyal clients. Something was wrong. Licking her lips, Lania continued to finish up her set so she could make her way back to Trigga's office and try her best to ease his mind.

"Nigga, why you just callin' us?" Gunplay yelled through the phone once he answered Trigga's call. "We still sitting out here in the middle of shitland waiting for your message, and you tellin' me you at the muthafuckin' club already? I got my whole damn crew out here! This some bullshit, Trigga. What kind of fuckin' time you on right now?"

Sitting at his desk, Trigga exhaled heavily and tried to get his thoughts together. His first thought had been to slide over to the house and snatch Keisha up by her throat but it was the middle of the night and he didn't want to do anything to Keisha in front of Cameron.

Reaching in his pocket, he pulled out the balled up picture and stared at it once more, trying once more to see if he could figure out who the man with Keisha was. He couldn't pick up on anything but that wasn't a problem. Once he paid Keisha a visit, she would tell him exactly what he wanted to hear.

"Somethin' fucked up happened while I was out there and I had to get the hell out. My bad, fam. But them niggas never showed up," Trigga replied back, trying to keep his tone even.

The line was silent for a while and Trigga knew Gunplay was trying to decide whether or not he wanted to ask more about the situation.

"Aye, I'm not alone so I'ma hit you up when I get to the crib. But you gone have to run this shit by me so don't even start with that close-mouthed shit you be on. I had all my hittas out there waiting to wreck some shit for your ass. I need some answers."

"And you will get them," Trigga told him just as there was a knock on the door. "I'll hit you back later."

Hanging up the phone, Trigga sighed and tried to neutralize his expression before getting up to open the door. When he saw Lania's face on the other end, he wasn't even surprised. If he were honest with himself, he had to admit that he was actually somewhat relieved to see her.

Although he hadn't noticed her when he first walked into the club, it was obvious she'd just finished dancing because there was a slight sheen of sweat on her face and her cheeks were flustered red. Her eyes held a concerned expression as they bore into Trigga's gray ones and he was slightly put off by the fact that he couldn't seem to pull his focus from off of her.

"Come in," he said, turning quickly around to break their stare. "You here to update me on what's been goin' on?"

"No, I came to check on you. Something's wrong and I can tell. Just tell me... is something going on at home?" she pried without shame before nudging the door closed behind her.

Incensed with anger that came all of a sudden, Trigga' eyes flared and hardened on Lania. She shifted her weight and sucked in a breath as she saw the sudden change in him as his anger set in.

"What da fuck I told you 'bout askin' me about shit that doesn't fuckin' concern you?! Your job is to take care of my club. If it doesn't have shit to do with what's goin' on in here, don't fuckin' ask about it," he snapped with a husky tone.

His tall, slim frame loomed over her, casting a shadow over her face as he snarled down over her with the edges of his lips pulled into a sneer.

Lania's mouth pulled into a tight line and her eyes became enflamed, matching his rage. It didn't take long for her to become just as pissed as he was. No man had ever treated her the way he had since he first met her but after her role increased around the club, she thought they were making progress towards something greater, especially after she'd picked him up the other day and patched up the gash in his side. But now here he was, once again acting like an asshole for no reason.

"You came in the club lookin' like you were fuckin' ran over, pushed through all of our customers without sayin' shit. You were rude as hell!" Lania shot back, walking in closer to Trigga. "So you're right... your personal shit doesn't concern me but *I'm* the one that built this club back up even past what it was when I started. So if your personal shit is fuckin' up what I did, then it *is* my business!"

After Lania finished fuming, she leaned forward and placed both of her hands on Trigga's desk while shooting daggers from her eyes to his. With a blank look on his face, Trigga watched her intently, somewhat shocked at her sudden outburst, Then he suddenly remembered something and his attention dropped to where her hands were on the table. He suddenly flinched before looking away and it was then that Lania looked down at his desk and saw it.

Right beneath her left hand was a crumpled up photo of Keisha hugging another man. She couldn't see much from the photo but she could tell the man definitely wasn't Trigga. Reaching down, she tried to grab it up but Trigga snatched it from her hands and stuffed it into his pocket.

"You think it's alright for you to go ahead and backpedal the fuck out of my business now?" he asked coarsely and Lania gave him a sympathetic look although, inside, she was cheering and trying to stop herself from jumping for joy.

"I'm sorry, Trigga," she lied in a way that seemed so genuine that Trigga felt his stomach clench from her sympathy. "I really am."

Trigga didn't say a word but he didn't have to. She could see the devastated look in his eyes because he was no longer trying to hide it. She already knew what was up between he and Keisha so there was nothing left to hide.

Walking over to where he stood unable to look her in her face, Lania placed her arms around him, wrapping him up in a hug. Her bare chest pressed against his body and, although Trigga didn't move to embrace her back, he couldn't help but be acutely aware of the way her naked body felt pressed against his. Shaking her away, Trigga took a shaky step back, increasing the distance between them.

"That's out of line," he told her but his tone didn't match his face. His face told her that he craved the touch of a woman, especially one who seemed to be concerned with only making him feel better after being hurt so badly. But his tone said that he was still trying, desperately to be faithful to his wife. And he was. As much as he wanted to be mad at Keisha for whatever it was she was doing, he couldn't make his body betray her.

Ignoring his words, Lania stepped forward and slipped her hand into his pants, expertly pulling out the bulge that lay beneath. Trigga shifted to object but she knew that he was only doing it because it was the right thing to do and not because he wanted to so she held her grip and moved quickly.

"The fuck are you—"

He swiped at her to knock her away but she was too fast and too focused. Before Trigga could even finish his sentence, she had placed the fullness of him between her jaws and was working his pole masterfully, swallowing it down like she'd pulled out all of her teeth. His girth surprised her and his length excited her. He was definitely everything that she'd expected him to be in more. Servicing him was a pleasure.

Lania sucked hard while she ran her tongue around the edge of his mushroom head, humming with pleasure as she completed the task that she hoped would be the start of their affair. Trigga was frozen in place, overcome with pleasure and completely void of any energy he needed in order to make her stop.

"Fuck... you gotta stop," he moaned but he made no movement to push her away.

His mind was conflicted and so was his heart. He loved Keisha but his head was a wreck and she was the cause. He knew that didn't excuse what was going down at the moment but he reasoned with himself that he was only letting Lania suck his dick. He wouldn't fuck her... wouldn't allow himself to betray Keisha in that way, so it couldn't be *that* bad.

"Shit..." Trigga moaned and then placed his hand behind Lania's head, pushing her forward in a rhythmic motion, aiding her in her task of nearly swallowing him whole. She complied happily, slobbing him down like there was no greater meal on Earth. If you could make love through your lips by way of your tongue, this was it.

Gritting his teeth, Trigga pushed her down hard, forcing his dick straight down her throat as he came, shooting his hot liquid straight down her the back of her esophagus. Lania swallowed it down like a pro and continued sucking, squeezing every last bit of his seed into her. She gulped it down like it was a milkshake and then pulled away, licking her lips and craving more.

When she stood up, she looked at Trigga and could tell by his eyes that the guilt was already starting to set in. She needed to make her exit quickly, before he got a chance to blame her for what he clearly saw as an indiscretion against his wife.

"I need to go check on the girls," Lania offered as she walked towards the door and unlocked it. Trigga hadn't even seen her lock it in the first place. If he had, he'd known then that she was up to no good when she first came in.

"Let me know if you need anything," she whispered before ducking out and closing the door behind her.

Running his hand over his face, Trigga sighed before sitting down in his seat and dropping his head in his hands. He was off his game in every way possible. For five years he'd succeeded at being the type of nigga that he and Gunplay had called lame back in the day; one who wasn't in the streets and wasn't concerned with nothing but loving and providing for his family. Back in the day, he and Gunplay would laugh and poke fun at men who were like the ones he'd become. They would call them easy targets.

But for five years, Trigga had been just that and was now even failing at it. He craved the dangerousness of the streets and the feeling it brought but he'd been gone too long. And now, being in the streets for only a short while was costing him his marriage. He didn't know who Keisha had been all hugged up on or why but he was going to find out. And, after that, he'd have to figure out this new situation with Lania.

21

I can't keep lying to Trigga like this, Keisha thought as she drove towards the restaurant where she would be meeting the man who had changed her entire life.

For the past couple weeks since Trigga had been gone, she'd been happier than she'd been in a long time. The stress of dealing with her changing body and the child they'd lost had been getting to her. But now, she was just starting to feel like her old self and she could thank Ishmael for that. He'd given her hope where she'd had none before. He was enriching her life in a way that she hadn't thought was possible. The only thing was... she was growing tired of lying to Trigga about what was going on and she knew that she couldn't keep doing it. It had already been so long. After kicking Trigga out, it made it easier but it left their relationship in an odd space that she hadn't thought would happen. It was time to come clean about everything.

"Hello?" Keisha said, answering her cellphone from inside her car without even looking at the number. The voice on the other end came in low, barely above a whisper, as the caller proceeded to speak with a wavering tone.

"Hi, um... Mrs. Blevins? This is Rebecca from—"

"I know where you're calling from," Keisha interrupted, feeling her heart began to race although she didn't know why. "Is everything okay with Cam? Why are you calling me?"

"Well, I—I'm calling because he's...he's not here."

Smashing on her brakes in the middle of the road, Keisha's car came to a sudden stop as a trail of cars behind her followed suit, slamming on their horns to sound off their discontent at her abrupt halt. Ignoring everything around her, Keisha focused all of her attention on the call.

"WHAT DO YOU *MEAN* HE'S NOT THERE?!" she screamed as the icy cold fingers of panic wound around her throat. She gasped for breath as she continued to speak. "I brought him to you this morning! I handed him over to his teacher directly. What do you mean my son is not there?!"

"I'm so sorry, ma'am," the woman started again, the panic in her own tone quite obvious. "I mean... his class went out for recess but he wasn't back when they came in. It was over an hour ago and we've looked everywhere since then—"

"An *hour* ago?! My baby has been missing for a fuckin' hour and you're just now telling me?!" Keisha screamed as she gripped so hard on the steering wheel, her knuckles went white. "I gotta find Trigga... oh God, my baby is missing... I gotta find Trigga."

Gasping for air, Keisha leaned her head on the steering wheel and said a quick prayer that this was all a misunderstanding and that Cameron was safely with his father.

"Ma'am, I—"

"You need to search every muthafuckin' corner you got in that fuckin' school right now! Lock all that shit down. If I hear about anybody moving in or out of that school, I'ma come down and personally kick your ass! You better find my baby before I find your dumb ass, you hear me?!"

Hanging up the phone, Keisha didn't even wait for Rebecca to respond because she didn't care one bit about what she had to say beyond her calling back to say she found Cameron. Trigga's was the next number she dialed. Keisha let it ring continuously until the voicemail picked up and then she called right back again. Still, there was no answer.

"SHIT!" Keisha cursed as she did an illegal U-turn in the middle of the road and started speeding down the street. She was only about three minutes away from the club and she prayed he was there.

Walking into the club, Keisha ignored everything and everyone around her and made a beeline straight to Trigga's office. Once she approached the door, she lifted her fist and pounded into it over and over again but no one answered. Finally, she felt a hand on her shoulder.

"Keesh... he's not in there," a voice said from beside her. It was Tory. With tears in her eyes that she could no longer hold back, Keisha whipped around to stare at her, noticing the way that Tory's eyes fell away. She seemed riddled with guilt about something. She couldn't even look in Keisha's face.

"Where is he? I need to see him..." Keisha asked, the tears now falling freely down her face.

Tory bit her lip like she didn't want to speak and it let Keisha know that wherever Trigga was and whatever he was doing was not something that she wanted to know. But she needed him. Whatever he was up to could be dealt with later. Right now, she needed to find her son.

"Tory, it's important! Speak, dammit! This is about my son! My son is missing," Keisha cried, wiping her palms over her face.

"Oh my God, Keisha, I'm so sorry! Oh my God." Tory's own eyes started to get misted with tears. "Trigga... is with Lania."

The hole in Keisha's chest grew larger as she processed Tory's words. Her entire world was crashing from around her. Everything was suddenly going from sugar to shit.

"What?"

"H—He's giving her a ride home... or at least that's what he told me...Her car isn't working," Tory continued, seeming more and more awkward with every word she uttered. Keisha shook her head as her eyes rose to the ceiling. Then she stared directly at Tory with piercing eyes.

"You have her number?" Keisha asked and Tory nodded her head. "Call her."

Without hesitation, Tory walked back down the hall towards the locker room with Keisha hot on her heels. Keisha watched, nearly without blinking, as Tory walked over to her locker and pulled her phone out of her purse. As soon as she went to Lania's number and pressed 'call', Keisha grabbed the phone.

"Hello?" Lania answered on the second ring.

"Bitch, hand the muthafuckin' phone over to *my* husband," Keisha ordered, her voice sharp as a knife. Lania chuckled a little which set Keisha's blood on fire and then there was a shuffling noise followed by muffled voices. She'd covered up the speaker to talk to Trigga.

I can't wait until this shit is over and I find my baby because I'ma beat the monkey shit out of her ass, Keisha thought to herself as she waited for Trigga to answer. *And then Trigga will be next.*

"Keesh?"

As soon as his voice came on the line, it calmed her, even in the midst of all that they had going on. She knew that all she had to do was tell him what was going on and he would solve everything for her. He could find Cameron.

"Trigga, I need you to meet me at Cam's school NOW!"

"Why—what's going on, Keisha?" he asked, the instant alarm in his voice putting Keisha on edge.

"He's missing. The school called me and said that he was gone!" she cried into the phone as fresh tears traveled down her eyes. The line went silent on the other end and Keisha's heart came to a complete stop until she heard Trigga's next words.

"I'll be there in five minutes," was all he said, his voice flat and void of emotion. But Keisha knew her husband and she knew that was how he was. In extreme situations of urgency, he kept his emotions at bay so that he could fall into action. For some reason, she sincerely believed with him involved that everything would be all right.

22

Oh my God, Lania thought to herself as they approached the school.

She was in a panic but she was trying her hardest to not give herself away. Not that Trigga was paying any attention to her anyways. Trigga hadn't said a single word to her since he got off the phone with Keisha but he didn't have to. Lania had heard every single word spoken. Right after hanging up the phone, he took a turn and started heading in a direction away from her apartment so she knew that he was going to his son's school.

Grabbing her cellphone, she glanced over at Trigga for a second before pecking out a message.

Do you have their son? she texted and waited for a reply.

But after about three minutes of waiting, she erased the message and pushed the phone back into her pocket. Still, she was on edge. This wasn't part of the plan and she wanted out. She didn't want to have anything to do with anyone's child being harmed. In fact, she'd wanted out of the plan even before Cameron's kidnapping. She had already decided that she wanted more. She wanted Trigga for her own.

"Stay in the car," was all Trigga said as he swerved into the parking lot of the school.

Before Lania could say a word, he jumped out and ran towards where Keisha was standing, speaking to another woman with her hands cupped around her mouth. Even though she felt bad for the son being gone, Lania couldn't help rolling her eyes at the sight of Keisha. She was beautiful, that was true. But she wasn't worthy enough to have someone like Trigga. What woman could stress a man like him? He loved her more than life and all she gave him was hell on Earth.

Trigga often spoke of their past and everything they'd gone through together but from what Lania could see, all that was behind them and now Keisha was simply a whiny ass female who wouldn't let Trigga be the man he needed to be. She was a control freak who didn't know how to let go when she had a good man.

Even now as Lania watched, Keisha was giving Trigga the business as if he wasn't also devastated at the fact that it was his son that was lost. From where Lania sat, she could see Keisha yelling and waving her arms in the air, pointing her index finger into his chest as she cried and screamed, making a public spectacle of them both. The white lady next to her had turned her body away from them, trying to give them some privacy, although everyone around them wasn't even bothering to pretend not to watch as Keisha yelled. Lania rolled down her window a bit so she could hear the feud.

"You better find my son! This is *all* your fault. I told you not to get back in the game but you did anyways and now our baby is gone!" Keisha yelled as tears fell down her eyes.

Biting down hard on his bottom lip, Trigga maintained his stoic expression in the midst of Keisha's outburst but didn't say a word. As Cameron's mother, it was her job to be emotional. But as his father, it was Trigga's job to figure out who had taken him and to handle it the best way he knew how. The *only* way he knew. If Keisha thought he was going to give up the streets before, she definitely knew he wouldn't now. There was no way he would ever be caught slipping again.

"There are no cameras on the playground?" Trigga asked, cutting his eyes to the flustered white woman standing next to them. Tears were rolling down her own cheeks, most likely because of the fact that she knew her job would be gone by morning. Keisha had already told her that she would be sure of that.

"No... but there were three teachers on the playground at that time and none of them saw anyone else there who wasn't supposed to be there. There were no other adults. I—I—just don't know how this happened!" she heaved out in distress as she tried to avoid Trigga's eyes. "The police are already checking the school again but—"

Trigga's phone vibrated in his pocket and he grabbed it, eager to see whom it was contacting him and hoping that it had something to do with

Cameron. When he was able to finally open the message, his stomach knotted up and his blood went ice cold. He was glad that Keisha was too busy crying to see his expression because he knew it would have been a dead giveaway. It was a photo of his son, wrapped up and bound by the ankles and wrists. He'd been crying, which was evident by his red-rimmed eyes.

What do you want? Trigga quickly texted back.

"He's not here," Trigga said, cutting the woman off. "Pull all surveillance from around the school. I want to see it all."

Although Trigga's face was void of expression, Keisha knew that something had happened to change Trigga's vibe. She could sense the shift although he wasn't saying anything and was making sure to avoid her eyes.

"Okay... I'll pull all the video and get back to you shortly," the woman said before turning around to walk away. Trigga allowed his eyes to follow her, refusing to look at Keisha.

"You *know* something," she accused him with her index finger raised, pointing him nearly right in the face. "You *know* something about what has happened to our son but you don't want to tell me! Is he alive?"

Sighing, Trigga looked at his wife, his heart aching as he witnessed her distress. She looked nothing like her normal self. The worry lines in her forehead were so deep that the appearance of them aged her a few years. Her eyes held dark spots around them that resembled a raccoon. She was torn and there was nothing he could do.

Remembering that Lania was in his car still, Trigga made the mistake of glancing behind him to see if she was still there. Keisha followed his stare and, as soon as he saw Keisha's eyes focus on where Lania was sitting, Trigga knew he'd really fucked up.

"You brought *her* here with you?" Keisha spat her words out at Trigga like venom as fresh tears came to her eyes. "This is all her fault and you *brought* her here?"

"I was taking her home when you called—"

"That bitch is the reason our son is missing, Trigga! This is *all* her fault but you're too busy fuckin' her to see it!" Keisha screamed to the top of her lungs.

The school was fairly empty apart from a few parents sprinkled about waiting to pick up their children. At this new twist in the script, all of them gawked at Keisha and Trigga with wide eyes as they digested the new information concerning Trigga and 'his whore'. Whispers erupted around them as the parents murmured their opinions to each other while keeping their eyes and ears open for any new developments.

"This is not the fuckin' time to be worried about another bitch, Keesh," Trigga said through his teeth as he began to get more and more agitated. "Our son is missing and I'm tryin' to focus on that. *Not* your fuckin' jealousy about another bitch."

Reaching out, Keisha pushed him out of the way and began storming towards his car. "Well, you need to focus on the bitch who knows what happened to him!"

"Keisha!" Trigga called out but he was too late.

In less than three seconds, Keisha had not only reached his car, but had pushed her hand through the open window and grabbed Lania by the hair. By the time Trigga was able to reach them, Keisha was catapulting punch after punch into Lania's face as the woman flung her arms around, trying to distance herself from Keisha from her awkward angle.

"You set all this shit up and I know you did, bitch! The shootout and all was you! Now tell me where the fuck is my son!" Keisha fumed as she delivered punch after punch.

Grabbing her up in a bear hug, Trigga caged Keisha between his arms and pulled her back but she kept her grip on Lania's hair. Lania opened her mouth and let out a shrill scream as Keisha pulled a few of her strands from the root before letting go.

"Calm the fuck down, Keesh!" Trigga gritted as he held her tightly in his arms, so tight that it hurt. Keisha twisted and reared back, trying to get free but he wouldn't let up. Eventually she gave up altogether and collapsed in a fit of tears. That's when Trigga finally let her go. Keisha fell straight to the ground, crumpling her body up like a small child as she sobbed into her hands.

"You need to calm the fuck down and let me handle this shit! You don't know what the fuck is goin' on but you always wanna jump into shit head first. Take your ass home, Keisha!" Trigga roared as he grabbed her by her arm and pulled her off the ground. Walking to her car, he placed Keisha inside and closed the door behind her.

"Go home because that's where our son will be looking for you."

And with that, Trigga turned around to address Lania and send her on her way. But when he looked inside of the car, he saw that she'd handled the job for him. She was already gone.

23

"**T**ake a left right here, please," Lania told the Uber driver once she jumped into his ride.

After being attacked by Keisha, Lania knew she had to get the fuck out of there because Keisha had said something that threw her for a loop.

You set all this shit up and I know you did, bitch! The shootout and all was you!

How did Keisha know that Lania had anything to do with the shootout at the club? And how did she know that she knew something about Cameron's kidnapping? She was getting her information from somewhere because it was too much of a coincidence. And once she explained it all to Trigga, Lania knew he would start investigating whether it was valid or not. So she had to get the hell out of dodge. But first, she needed to check with someone to make sure her escape plan was sound.

"I'll get out right here," Lania said, jumping out of the car.

With her small purse in her hand, she darted across the parking lot of the hotel and ran straight in, bumping into a few other guests in the process. She ignored their remarks of how rude she was being and pressed on through the lobby, slipping into the elevator just in a knick of time. Jamming her finger on the button for her desired floor, she closed her eyes and waited as the elevator soared upwards.

"Long day, huh?" a voice said across from her. She opened her eyes and gave a curt smile at the older white man who stood next to her.

Nodding her head, she replied, "It definitely has. I can't wait for it to be over."

The man smiled once more and nodded his head as the elevator stopped. Tossing her a small wave he walked off and Lania was grateful to finally be alone. She searched through her purse for the keycard that she'd been given and pulled it out. She knew that he wouldn't like for her to pop on up him but she didn't have a choice. She'd called and texted but he wasn't answering his phone. Now this was an emergency situation and she had to get the fuck out of dodge. But she had nowhere to go. He was all she had left if Trigga turned on her.

The elevator dinged and she stepped off, wiping a thin line of sweat off her lip as she dashed down the hall. Once she finally reached his room she let out a sigh of relief and pressed the keycard into the lock. The green light lit up and the lock clicked. She pushed the door open and stormed in.

The undeniable sound of lovemaking was the first thing she picked up upon entering the room and her heart dropped as she froze in place. No, it wasn't lovemaking. It was the undeniable sound of *fucking*. Somebody was getting it in to the max. From the sounds of it, whoever it was, he was putting a hurting on the female because she was wailing in a combination of pain and pleasure as he pushed so hard into her that the headboard was knocking against the wall.

It can't be him, Lania thought as she finally attempted to move her feet towards the sound.

But it was like she was standing in quicksand. She couldn't lift her feet, couldn't walk towards the sound. She simply stared down the hall as it continued on, waiting for some confirmation that it wasn't *her* man having sex with another woman. Not after all that she'd done for him. Not after he sent her here to get to know another man so that he could creep in and find a way to expand into New York. No, it couldn't possibly be *her* man in there fuckin' another bitch.

And so with that thought in mind, Lania unglued her feet and walked steadily down the hall towards the room and stepped right in the open door.

"AUSTIN?!" she yelled as tears came to her eyes.

Austin, so caught up in his moment, didn't bother to even turn around. He just continued to beat into the woman's guts as if Lania wasn't there. Lania's mouth dropped as he watched him plummet his massive, muscular and god-like body forward into another woman's throbbing wet pussy. Neither one of them seemed to know that she was there and Lania had begun to think that maybe she hadn't spoke at all until Austin turned in her direction, glancing for only a second, before biting down on his bottom lip and humping harder into the dark-skinned beauty on the bed.

This wasn't the first time that Austin had cheated on her but in the past she'd given him a reason to. Like Keisha, she'd made the mistake of not appreciating the man that she had and he'd stepped out to find a substitute. But what bothered her now was that she'd done everything he asked, *anything* he needed in order to keep him and he was still back to his same old games. But *this time* he didn't even seem to care that he'd been caught.

Unsure of what to do, Lania was about to walk back out of the room and wait until Austin was done before demanding that he send her home but something stopped her. It was the woman. Something seemed a little too familiar about her. She'd stopped screaming and moaning once Lania had announced her presence but there was something else about her that Lania recognized. Walking around slowly, Lania focused her attention on the woman that Austin was ferociously humping into and then gasped when her eyes met her face.

"KARMEN?!" Lania screamed but it wasn't from the same emotion that she'd felt when she saw Austin. This time, the only thing she felt was pure hate as she watched her best friend getting dicked down by the first man she'd ever loved.

Reaching out, Lania took a play from Keisha's book and grabbed Karmen by her long black hair. She tugged so hard that Austin fell backwards, detaching his dick from Karmen's pussy with a loud sopping sound as Lania jumped onto her, slamming punches at every space on Karmen's body that she could connect with. Never in a million years would she have been prepared for this. Karmen had been her friend since before she'd even met Austin. She'd always been the one giving her advice on how to handle it whenever he went away for long amounts of times or even how to deal with it when he was cheating on her.

But the more that Lania thought about it, Karmen's advice had always led to her doing something that would piss Austin off or distance her from him, like when she advised her to fuck Trigga. And most times when Austin was out of town, so was Karmen, stating that she was going to visit her grandmother or cousins. The two of them had been fucking around for quite some time.

"Get the fuck off me!" Karmen yelled as she delivered a strong blow to Lania's face that knocked her backwards into the wall.

From there, Karmen jumped on top of her and pinned her down to the point that she couldn't move as she continued her assault. Karmen was much thicker than Lania was and the extra weight helped her easily take control of the fight.

"Stop this stupid shit," Austin said and plucked Karmen's body from off of Lania's like she weighed no more than a feather.

She continued thrashing and kicking the entire time. One hit connected with Lania's jaw and Lania groaned as blood filled her mouth. But she couldn't even register the pain from that. She was so utterly hurt by the betrayal at the hands of the only two people in the world that she thought she could depend on.

"Lania what the fuck you actin' like this for? You know I fuck other bitches," Austin continued as he stood over her, watching her mop up the blood on her face with her forearm. "What the fuck I do with my dick don't concern you. And it damn sure don't concern you, Karmen. Get the fuck up, Lania. Actin' like this shit is brand new to you. You know how I do."

Shaking her head, Lania cried as she began to speak.

"I didn't know you were doin' this shit, Austin! I—I..."

"Well, then you're stupid," Austin replied harshly while chuckling. His laugh sounded like sandpaper rubbing against her ears.

"A nigga like me always got more than one bitch. You my favorite because you do everything I need you to do without talking shit. And in return I give you every fuckin' thing you can ask for," Austin said as he looked down at her, his handsome face, the one that she'd easily fallen in love with years ago, was now snarling down at her like she was garbage.

His blue eyes had a speckle of green and brown in the middle, which only surfaced when he was at his deadliest. Lania bit her bottom lip to stop herself from crying out or saying anything else that would infuriate him. She knew Austin well enough to know that once his dark side took over, she needed to retreat. Apparently, Karmen hadn't been messing with him for long enough to know.

"What you mean she your favorite?! I thought that we—"

WHAP!

A long, low cry escaped from Karmen's lips after Austin slapped her hard against the side of her face, sending her sailing backwards until she fell onto the bed. She lay flat, pulling her arms around her knees and shrunk away from him as he stood over her, wondering whether or not she needed to be hit once more. When blood began to rush from between her lips, it was then that he was satisfied.

"What da fuck are you doin' here, Nia? I didn't call your ass!" Austin bellowed, returning his attention to her. Lania's bottom lip trembled as she looked into his eyes to speak. Seeing the callousness of his gaze, she turned away.

"I was calling you but you didn't answer. I—I was trying to see what was happening... Trigga's son was kidnapped and—you didn't say anything about taking his kid!"

"Why the fuck you actin' like this shit is a surprise to you?" Austin countered as he squat down so that she was staring right into his face. "You know why the fuck we here and what we are supposed to do! I'ma hit that nigga in every way I can so I can get what I want from his ass!"

Sobbing, Lania couldn't hold back her cries any longer as she listened to Austin speak. This wasn't according to plan. She drew the line at messing with someone's kids, especially Trigga's kid.

"But he has what you wanted... he tried to meet you today with the money but you—"

"You think this shit is about a few fuckin' dollars?" Austin asked, pressing his face so close to Lania that she could feel the heat from his breath on her face. "This shit ain't about no fuckin' money! Trigga is they key for me to connect with what I need to spread my name farther than it's ever been. By the time I'm through I'll own muthafuckin' New York and every muthafucka in it. This ain't about no few dollars! But you too stupid to see that shit."

Austin's words stopped the tears from coming down Lania's face as she realized that she wasn't Austin's partner at all. She was merely a pawn that he was using to help with carrying out his major plan. He hadn't told her the whole story of what he planned to do and she had been too stupid to realize it. But it made sense. Austin made hundreds of thousands of dollars a day just off of running the dope game now that he was supreme in Texas and Atlanta, where he'd taken over his cousin, Lloyd's, empire. He was even moving in on Miami, which would almost double his current worth. Of course he didn't just want a few million from Trigga. He wanted it all. And according to Austin, Trigga was the key. But how?

"Get the fuck out of here," Austin said, finally standing up and turning away from Lania. "I'll call you when I need your stupid ass. Until then... stay gone and take care of my fuckin' kids."

Lania stood up slowly, dragging her feet as she thought about what Austin had said. He'd lied to her the entire time. He was out for more and by the time he was done, Trigga would be dead.

"You didn't hurt him, did you? Did you hurt his son?" Lania asked, turning around just as she approached the door.

"What the fuck you care?" Austin growled as he glared at her. "And you better keep your fuckin' mouth closed. Because if that nigga finds out you're involved, he'll do much worse to our kids. So get your fuckin' mind right before I do it for you."

With Austin's cold threat still echoing in her ears, Lania walked out and closed the door behind her. She couldn't deny that she had feelings for Trigga and she couldn't deny that she didn't want him or his son harmed but she had to look out for self first.

24

———————

*S*itting in her car, surrounded by people who were laughing and going about their day as if there was nothing wrong in the world, Keisha watched the entrance of the hotel Lania had ran into with tears streaming down her eyes. She didn't care what Trigga said; deep in her heart she knew that her instincts were right. Yadi had said she heard Lania on the phone the day of the shootout and she'd believed her instantly when she said that she couldn't be trusted. This wasn't just blind jealousy; this was a woman's intuition. Lania had something to do with Cameron's kidnapping.

When Trigga placed her in the car and told her to leave, it was the last thing she had in mind to do. Until she saw Lania running across the street looking like she had something to hide. Without batting an eye in Trigga's direction, Keisha took off after Lania and then trailed her all the way to the hotel. But after about ten minutes of sitting there, she began to panic. What if Trigga was right about her being home? That was the place that Cameron would expect his family to be. If he was lost and anyone found him, he'd give out the address to their home. She needed to be there in case he showed up.

"What the hell am I doing?" Keisha muttered as she wiped the tears from her face and placed the car into drive. She was focusing on the wrong things. Caught up in what Trigga had going on with another woman and trying to convince herself that it was for Cameron. But it wasn't. She needed to be home waiting for her baby to return. Because he *would* return.

Just as Keisha was about to pull out of her parking space, she looked up and saw Lania running out of the hotel doors. She had her hands over her face as she took off across the parking lot. Keisha stared at her intently and realized she was crying. A nagging feeling tugged at the nape of Keisha's neck as she watched Lania continue to run down the road where she eventually hailed a cab. Something wasn't right and, although her mind was telling her to leave, her instincts were saying that she was close to something big. She needed to see what Lania was up to before she left. She couldn't risk missing out on something that would bring her closer to finding her son.

Shutting off the car, Keisha stepped out of the car and wiped away the remnants of tears from her face as she dashed forward towards the building, unsure of what she would find or how she would find it. She didn't even know what she was looking for. It was obvious that Lania had been visiting someone but how would she figure out who that was?

"How may I help you, ma'am?" the concierge asked her as she walked in the building. Her eyes darted left and right, searching for any sign of Cameron anywhere. The foyer and adjoining restaurant was littered with people and even small children. But none of them looked like her son.

"Um..." Keisha said as she teetered slowly to the concierge, a petite, blond woman who appeared to be in her early thirties or maybe late twenties. Keisha wondered if she was a mother. Pulling up a photo of Cameron on the screen of her phone, she held it in front of the woman's face.

"Have you seen this boy? He's my son..." Tears came to her eyes and she tried to blink them away. "H—he was taken from school this morning and I thought he might have been brought here."

The woman's eyes shot wide open as she listened to Keisha's words before darting over to the photo on the screen. Squinting, she stared at the image for a long while but Keisha already knew the truth. She could read it in her expression. She hadn't seen Cameron or, if she did, she couldn't recall it.

"He was taken from school... did someone say they saw him here? Was he brought here?" the woman asked. Her eyes were still tight at the ends as she peered at the image on Keisha's phone, desperately wanting to help her although she was unable to.

"No... it's okay," Keisha sniffled as she placed the phone in her pocket. "He's not here."

"Ma'am, I'm sorry I—"

Keisha turned away at the same time that the elevator chimed from across the lobby. She wiped at her eyes, preparing to give up and walk back to her car, feeling completely defeated by her failure at finding anyone or anything to help in locating her son. But after taking a single step forward, she lifted her head and her eyes fell on a couple walking off the elevator.

The woman was a beautiful shade of mocha brown with long black hair that she had pulled high into a long ponytail. She had a smile on her face that spoke volumes about what she must have felt inside: that she was the luckiest girl in the world because of the man she had by her side. She was elegant in all of her designer clothing that obviously cost thousands of dollars, or maybe it was the way she wore them that gave off that impression.

But it was the man by her side that made all of the blood drain from Keisha's face. It was almost like seeing a ghost, no a demon. All of the feelings that Keisha had tucked away over the last five years came to the surface as she froze in place and stared at the man who was a walking memorial of all the things she prayed at night to forget.

Austin? Keisha questioned in her mind, as if asking instead of stating would make it not so.

But he was there... in the flesh. There was Lloyd's cousin. Suddenly stuck with the urge to pee, Keisha turned around just as they walked by her, neither one of them paying her the slightest bit of attention as they passed.

"Are we going shopping for baby clothes?" the woman asked happily as they passed by. The mention of baby clothes was like a stab in the gut for Keisha as she thought once again about Cameron.

"I mean, I don't know why you didn't just tell her that I was pregnant... then we don't have to keep playin' this little game with her—ow!" the woman howled but not loud enough to draw too much attention to herself. Keisha turned slightly to see what was happening and saw that Austin was holding her hand very tightly at an awkward angle to draw pain.

"Shut the fuck up," he said through his teeth, barely loud enough for Keisha to hear him. "You don't make the plans when it comes to this shit. I do."

The harshness in his tone brought tears to Keisha's eyes. He reminded her so much of his cousin and Keisha knew that his presence was not a coincidence. Neither was the fact that Lania had been running out of the very hotel that he was staying in. Austin was here for something and he was using Lania to do it. He was using her to get close to Trigga for a reason.

But why?

Keisha didn't realize that she was staring until she suddenly felt the heat of Austin's stare on her face. She turned away rapidly, closing her eyes and saying a prayer that he hadn't seen her.

Oh God, she thought as she froze in place, hoping that he hadn't recognized her. But somewhere deep down inside, she knew it was too good to be true.

"Ma'am, a—are you okay?" the concierge asked once more. Keisha had forgotten she was there.

"Yes... um," she started with a croaky tone. "Is there a back exit?"

"Yes, it's..."

While the woman rattled off the directions, Keisha glanced over to where Austin and his girlfriend had been but they were gone.

"Thank you!" Keisha whispered to the woman as she ran pass the elevators and through the restaurant, following the instructions to escape out the back door. Picking up her phone, she called Trigga and prayed that he would pick up.

"Trigga!" she yelled when she heard the phone stopped ringing. She didn't even wait for him to greet her. She needed to tell him about Austin as soon as possible because the dreaded feeling that something was about to happen was still upon her.

"Keesh? What's goin' on? You not at the house?"

Pausing for a minute, Keisha ducked into a booth so that she could finish the call before leaving the building. She checked around her for Austin but didn't see him anywhere. It was nearly impossible to miss his tall, muscular frame.

"No, listen...I followed Lania to a hotel—"

"What?! See, this what the fuck I'm talkin' about, Keesh! I told you to—"

"Trigga, listen! Just let me talk," Keisha cried into the phone, much louder than she had intended inside of the quiet restaurant. Dropping her voice to a whisper, she continued.

"I followed her here and... she was meeting Austin. He's here and he saw me..."

The line went silent and she closed her eyes as tears filled them. She hoped that the last interaction that she had with her husband wouldn't be the one from earlier with her accusing him of being with another woman and blaming him for their son's kidnapping. She hoped that her last interaction with her son wouldn't be how she dropped him off that morning, so stressed about everything that she forgot to kiss him goodbye. This couldn't be it. She had to be with her family again.

"Where are you?" Trigga asked with an even but frigid tone. She knew his coldness wasn't directed at her. He had a child missing and a wife in danger. He had a lot on his shoulders but she knew he would take care of it all. For the first time since they had parted, she finally had faith in him to do what he'd always done. Handle the situation and keep his family safe.

"I'll send you the address."

"Don't leave... stay wherever you are, make sure you're always surrounded by a group of people. *Don't* move and I'll be there," Trigga instructed. In the background, Keisha could already hear him shuffling around as he made moves to be with her. She knew that he was on his way and the thought calmed her.

"Okay, I will," she told him. "I love you."

"I love you too."

Wiping her face once more, Keisha hung up the phone just as a waiter came to her table. He peered at her with a curious expression on his face as if he were wondering about her story based on her disheveled appearance and tear-stained face.

"Can I get you anything to eat?" he asked and Keisha shook his head.

"No, but I'll take a glass of water... and some coffee," she added when she saw the judgmental look on his face at her just ordering a free glass of water. She couldn't eat and probably would barely be able to bring herself to drink.

"And where is your restroom?" Keisha asked right before he left. The man pointed to a pair of doors behind her and then walked away.

Sighing, Keisha stood up and trotted towards the women's restroom to freshen up. She was still worried sick about her son but she knew she had to pull it together so she could be a help to Trigga when he got there. After washing her face, she was going to call the police and see if they had any updates on Cameron. Then she was going to call Queen, if Trigga hadn't already. Queen was better than the police and, when it came to Cameron, there was probably no other woman who loved him just as much as Keisha did than Queen. With her help, they could find him.

Keisha was splashing water on her face when she heard the restroom door open but it was the sound of the lock clicking that surprised her. She rubbed the water from her eyes and gripped the edge of the sink as she turned towards the door. As soon as she turned, her face connected with what felt like an iron punch and she dropped to the floor gasping.

"Ugh!" Keisha moaned as she fell headfirst onto the tile floor in the bathroom.

Her vision was blurred as her mouth filled with blood. She tried to open it to yell but a surge of excruciating pain passed through her. It felt like her jaw was broken. The heavy sound of footsteps coming towards her placed her in a state of panic and she began to try to crawl away but was barely able to move an inch before her head was yanked backwards by her hair.

"Don't I know you?" Austin's icy voice chilled her to the bone as he spoke directly into her ear. The feel of his breath against her face only increased the pain she felt as he pulled harder on her hair, rearing her head back and nearly pulling her hair from the scalp. Sharp pains surged through her jaw, feeling as if it would split open at any moment.

"I want you to deliver a message to your husband from me," Austin cruelly informed her as he lifted his foot and delivered a blow to her side, kicking her straight in the gut.

In spite of the pain coming from her jaw, Keisha still opened her mouth to let out an ear-splitting scream but Austin cut it short with another punch to the face, silencing her. Grabbing her by the arms, he slammed her against the wall, knocking the wind from her lungs. Keisha fell forcefully to the ground; her entire body feeling like it's on fire as she fell into a fit of coughs.

Tears ran down her face and mixed with the blood there as she wallowed on the ground, unable to move a muscle. She couldn't open her eyes but she could see a dark, looming shadow above her, cutting off the light from above her eyelids. Fear crippled her body as she attempted to move out of the way but it was for no use. There was nowhere to go.

Lifting his fists, a smirk crossed Austin's face as he stared down at the beautiful, bloodied woman beneath him. It was a shame that he didn't have enough time to do what he really wanted to do to her. The fact that she had been able to have his cousin and Trigga, two of the most deadliest men he'd known, in love with her meant that she had to be working with gold underneath her clothes but he didn't have time to test her out.

Next time, he vowed as he began to pummel her with punches all over her body.

By the time her husband saw her, he wouldn't be able to recognize her and that's exactly how he wanted it. He needed to break Trigga down to the point that he would no longer resist and would fall into his plan. Austin had his eyes set on taking over Queen's empire and also moving in on Gunplay's stronghold on the city of New York. Trigga was the common piece in the middle of both of them. He had both of their trust. He could get Austin what he needed.

But the fact that Trigga thought he could play him by pulling Gunplay's team in on the money swap let him know that Trigga still wasn't ready to play the submissive role he needed him in. Trigga still thought that he could have the upper hand. It was time to break him down a little further.

"Shit... I know you ain't dead," Austin whispered as he looked down at Keisha's battered body on the ground beneath him.

Kicking his foot into her ribs, he huffed in relief when she whimpered from the pain of his subtle touch. Her buttery complexion was now a grayish blue and mired by blood. Smiling, he congratulated himself for a job well done. She looked nothing like herself.

"You can let him know that this is the kinda shit he can look forward to if he doesn't follow the plan," Austin told her as he straightened up his clothes and washed his hands.

"My son..." Keisha sputtered through her swollen and busted lips. It was the only thing she could utter and even doing so caused her an intense amount of pain but she needed to know about Cameron.

"What?" Austin asked, leaning down after shutting off the water. He placed his ear nearly on top of her lips. "What you say?"

"My son," Keisha repeated before sputtering out more bloody coughs.

"Oh," Austin grinned as he pulled away from her. "You wanna know about that ugly ass lil' boy of yours, huh?"

He paused and Keisha wanted to respond but she couldn't. Her ribs ached to the point that she could barely breathe. It felt like her chest was collapsing. Her breaths came out in painful wheezes. She couldn't say another word.

"He's dead," Austin said, freezing Keisha's heart. "Your son is dead."

And with that, he unlocked the door to the bathroom and walked out, closing it firmly behind him as Keisha let the pain overcome her. Her heart bled at hearing that her son was dead and the pain from the realization that he was gone hurt far worse than the damage to her body.

She didn't want to live anymore. She was done.

25

*B*y the time that Trigga got to the hotel, there was an ambulance as well as a fire truck and about five police cars pulled up in front of the building. No one had to tell him a thing. He knew they were there because of Keisha. His heart began to drum loudly in his ears as he ran over to the entrance, his eyes searching for any clue of what had happened to his wife.

"Daddy? What's wrong?" Cameron said by his side.

"Nothing," Trigga told him, although what he really wanted to say was 'everything'. *Everything* was wrong.

Just as he'd suspected, Cameron's kidnapping had been a warning from whom he now knew was Austin. Austin had taken Cameron to make a statement. He knew that Trigga had been trying to set him up at the money drop and he wanted to show Trigga that he was five steps ahead of him. While Trigga was waiting for the drop so that Gunplay and his team could swarm in and take over, Austin had showed that he could touch his family. First, Cameron and, now, Keisha.

Trigga had been right around the corner from the house when Keisha called him and was about to turn around to head straight to her until a neighbor called, telling him that Cameron was at his house. Apparently he'd been dropped off at home and no one was there so he went to the neighbor's. Trigga grabbed up his son, ensuring he was safe before heading to his wife. Now he was wondering if he'd made the right decision. Did those few minutes he spent getting Cameron cost Keisha her life?

"What happened?" Trigga asked one of the medics standing in front of the building. His chest was so tight, it was a wonder he could breathe. All he could think about was Keisha.

The medic, a young woman with smooth caramel skin was standing outside with a greenish look on her face like she was going to be sick. Her expression brought on the feeling of panic onto Trigga and it coursed quickly through his veins as he watched her, waiting for her to answer.

"A woman's in there," she started. "She's been beat really badly. S—she... it looks bad. It's only my first day on the job and..."

"She's my wife. Is she alive?" Trigga asked, his voice catching in his throat before he could say a word more.

The woman nodded her head very slowly, tears coming to her eyes. Her eyes darted around everywhere but Trigga's face as her mouth began to move.

"She is but... she's—" She stopped speaking once her eyes focused on Cameron who was standing by his father's side watching her face intensely, absorbing every single word.

Trigga looked around at all of the police officers standing around and then down at his son. He had to get in to see Keisha but he couldn't let him see his mother in the state she was in.

"Watch him, please," Trigga pleaded, placing Cameron's hand in the woman's. She nodded her head and looked at him affectionately. "Cam, stay here until I come out. Okay?"

With eyes stretched wide, Cameron nodded his head.

"I'll watch him," she told Trigga. "We'll be right here when you get back."

Apprehensively, Trigga trudged into the entrance of the hotel slowly, as if his feet were being held down in restraints. He wanted to see Keisha to make sure she was okay but he knew tit was useless. She was *not* okay. That much was evident from the young medic's face. What he really was about to see was how bad things really were. Would she make it through?

Straight in front of him, there was a group of medics along with a few police officers, all of them surrounding a stretcher. Trigga pushed forward with more strength, knowing that it was Keisha they were tending to.

"Sir, you can't come any closer," someone informed him but Trigga ignored the warning.

"That's my wife," he said as he continued to walk.

The voice turned to whisper to another person who whispered to another and soon there was a cacophony of sound around him. Voices saying words that he could not hear and didn't care to know. He just wanted to know that Keisha was all right.

But when he moseyed close enough to see her, Trigga's heart broke.

"That's not her," he said as he pushed closer and watched two medics as they strapped her body down to the stretcher. "That's not Keisha."

What lay in front of Trigga was not Keisha... at least that's what his mind told him. Her beautiful hair was clotted and matted with blood; her face was bruised and swollen beyond recognition. Her golden brown skin was a hue purplish-blue. Her lips were busted and her nose was dislocated. This was *not* her.

"That's not your wife?" someone said from beside him. It was the same voice from earlier.

A single tear came to Trigga's face but he blinked it away. The tear must have been enough of an answer to the man standing next to him because he turned to the medics strapping Keisha's body down and spoke.

"Hey! This man says he's her husband!"

Everyone around Trigga froze and sent sympathetic stares in his direction as he toddled closer, pressing on towards where Keisha lay, frozen and unmoving. He couldn't even tell if she was breathing.

"Keisha?" he whispered as he leaned into her.

"Sir... we gotta get her to the hospital. You can travel with us in the ambulance but we have to go NOW!" a medic said from his side but he ignored him. Then Keisha's lips began to move. She was trying to speak.

"C—Cam is..." she uttered in a coarse tone, which nearly brought Trigga to his knees. She was in so much pain and there was nothing he could do about it. He'd failed her. If only he'd gotten to her sooner, this never would have happened.

"Cam is fine. He was at the house. He's outside; I just didn't want him to see you like this. But I have him and he's fine," Trigga told her before biting down hard on his lips to stop his emotions.

Despite her pain, the edges of her bubbled and busted mouth twisted up in a partial smile. Tears slid down the corners of her eyes at the realization that Cameron was alright. The past few moments of feeling like her baby was dead had been the worst moments of her life.

"Sir, I'm going to need you to move," the medic grumbled again in a more forceful tone as he nudged Trigga out of the way. But Keisha's fingers stretched to where Trigga had placed his hand to her side and she poked down hard into his hand, stopping him. He froze and his attention went to her. Looking down, he saw her face twisting up in pain but her lips were moving. He leaned down close so he could hear her.

"Th—the ba-baby," she wheezed out. "The baby…"

Confused, Trigga's brows furrowed as he ran his eyes over Keisha's face, wondering why she was asking about Cameron again.

"He's fine, Keisha. Your baby is fine. Cam is outsi—"

But he stopped when Keisha brought his hand over to her pocket. Frowning, Trigga reached in and pulled out a piece of paper that was folded up inside.

"Okay, we *really* have to go. Step aside, sir," the medic ordered as they pushed past Trigga and pulled Keisha away.

Trigga stumbled after them while opening up the paper. It was a sonogram. According to the numbers typed in the right-hand corner, Keisha was just over eight weeks pregnant. Clenching his jaw tight, the realization of Trigga's current situation fell upon him. He'd saved one child but he may have just lost another.

"Sir, would you like to ride with us or follow behind?" the medic asked as he gave Trigga a look of urgency.

Shaking his head, Trigga unclenched his jaws and told him, "I have my son with me. I'll meet you there."

Walking out of the building, he looked over to where Cameron was standing with tears in his eyes. He didn't know what was going on but he knew it involved his mother and he was panicking. After the day he'd had, Trigga couldn't blame him.

"Daddy, is that mommy on the bed?" Cameron asked, still blinking away his tears.

Without answering, Trigga glanced at the woman holding his hand, giving her a nod of thanks and took Cameron's hand in his. As they walked towards the car, Cameron looked around but didn't ask his father about his mother again and Trigga was grateful for that. He didn't know how to explain to his son that someone had beaten his mother nearly to death or that his father was about to turn back into a killer.

Once Trigga sat behind the wheel after securing Cameron into his seat, his phone chimed. Gritting his teeth, he grabbed it up quickly and checked the message.

This is what happens when you think you can outsmart me, it read.

Despite his situation, Trigga began to laugh. But it was like a cruel, evil and maniacal chuckle; the kind one does right before killing someone in the cruelest of ways. Because that's exactly what he intended to do. Everyone who had anything to do with harming his family was about to feel more pain than they'd ever inflicted on him. Austin and anyone else involved.

"WHAT THE HELL are you doing calling this number?" the voice on the other end asked as Lania held the phone to her ear. Wiping away tears, she sniffled as she threw more clothes into her suitcase and then glanced at her children sitting on the bare mattress behind her.

"I didn't know who else to call! I have no one who can help me—"

"And you still have no one," the voice informed her, sounding cold as ice. "I gave you one job and you're already calling me crying. Is it that hard to get a man to want to fuck you? Is it that hard to break up a marriage that is already just about broken?"

Closing her eyes, Lania gritted her teeth in worry. She was running out of options and she had no one to turn to, which was the only reason she was even on the phone with this person in the first place. Deep down, she knew she wouldn't find help here but she had to try. She had no one else.

"You said that them being together affected your money, which was why you needed me. I did everything you asked! And I can continue to do more if you'd just help me," Lania pleaded, on the verge of breaking down into tears. "I'm almost there... some shit went down today but it's nothing I can't fix. I just need a little help. That's all."

There was a long pause on the other line and then, finally, she heard the words she wanted to hear.

"Fine. I'll help you only because I still need you. But it's only going to be this *one* time."

Shutting her eyes, Lania voiced a praise of thanks to God and then told the person what it was that she needed. From now on, she knew that she had to look out for herself because if Trigga knew what she'd done, he would be coming after her and wouldn't stop until she was dead.

Austin was on his own.

THE FINALE IS OUT NOW!

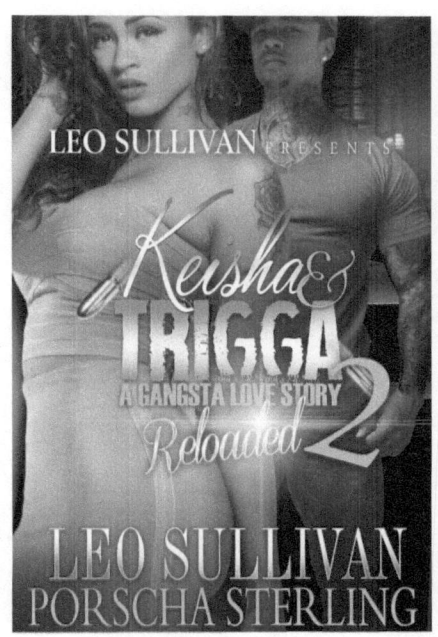

THANKS FROM PORSCHA

THANK YOU to the readers who support our team! We love you and appreciate you! Please connect with us on Facebook and definitely leave a review. We read them and take your input seriously. It's a great help to us, as authors, to know what you think and what you want from us.

Thank you to my #DOPEAUTHORS who make up ROYALTY PUBLISHING HOUSE! Y'all are amazing! I appreciate you ALL!

Thanks goes to my son, Al, and to Leo! Neither one of you will ever know how much I appreciate and love you! Leo, you inspire, mentor and motivate me. And, for that, I will always be grateful!

THE NEXT ONE IS COMING SOON! But in the meantime, as you wait, check out the books written by our authors. They are some of the most talented authors who have ever done it!

I hope you enjoyed this novel. Until we meet again...#StayRoyal

THANKS FROM LEO

First, I would like to thank God for, once again, allowing me to do what I have been blessed to do and that is writing and creating with my mind and capturing the vivid imagination of millions. I would also like to thank you, the readers, without you none of this could be possible. I would also like to thank my family, which are too many to name but I love you all!

Right now, some of the most important people in my life are the team of writers on my roster. I call them Family. Shoutout to the entire staff and writers at Sullivan Productions LLC Films and Literary. Also, I have to give props to my executive assistant, Tina.

I would be remiss if I didn't thank my very beautiful and talented co-writer, Porscha Sterling. For me, this has been a labor of love.

Thanks for the reviews, they motivate me to write. I read them all and if you tell me to hurry, I do my best. One thing is for sure, the next installment in this series will come soon... you won't have to wait long.

So until next time, peace and blessings.

You can follow me on Facebook or Instagram.

LEO SULLIVAN

READ MORE ON THE LIT READING APP!

Read more books like this one **for less**! Check out some other new releases on the LiT Reading App. Go to www.litreadingapp.com to learn more!

JOIN OUR MAILING LIST!

Text **LEOSULLIVAN** to **22828** to join our mailing list!
To submit a manuscript for our review, email us at
submissions@leolsullivan.com

To submit a manuscript for our review, email us at
leosullivanpresents@gmail.com